TIME HUNTER

-736

ECHOES

TIME HUNTER

ECHOES
by IAIN McLAUGHLIN
& CLAIRE BARTLETT

TELOS
.CO.UK

First published in England in 2005 by Telos Publishing Ltd
61 Elgar Avenue, Tolworth, Surrey, KT5 9JP, England - www.telos.co.uk
Telos Publishing Ltd values feedback. Please e-mail us with any comments
you may have about this book to: feedback@telos.co.uk

ISBN: 1-903889-45-6 (paperback)
Echoes © 2004 Iain McLaughlin and Claire Bartlett
ISBN: 1-903889-46-4 (deluxe hardback)
Echoes © 2004 Iain McLaughlin and Claire Bartlett
Time Hunter format © 2003 Telos Publishing Ltd. Honoré Lechasseur and
Emily Blandish created by Daniel O'Mahony.
The moral rights of the author have been asserted.

Typeset by Arnold T. Blumberg
& ATB Publishing Inc. (www.atbpublishing.com)

Printed in India

1 2 3 4 5 6 7 8 9 10 11 12 13 14 15

THE TIME HUNTER

Honoré Lechasseur and Emily Blandish ... Honoré is a black American ex-GI, now living in London, 1950, working sometimes as a private detective, sometimes as a 'fixer', or spiv. Now life has a new purpose for him as he has discovered that he is a time-sensitive. In theory, this attribute, as well as affording him a low-level perception of the fabric of time itself, gives him the ability to sense the whole timeline of any person with whom he comes into contact. He just has to learn how to master it.

Emily is a strange young woman whom Honoré has taken under his wing. She is suffering from amnesia, and so knows little of her own background. She comes from a time in Earth's far future, one of a small minority of people known as time channellers, who have developed the ability to make jumps through time using mental powers so highly evolved that they could almost be mistaken for magic. They cannot do this alone, however. In order to achieve a time-jump, a time channeller must connect with a time-sensitive.

When Honoré and Emily connect, the adventures begin.

DEDICATION

For the people who matter. You know who you are.

PROLOGUE

The tower loomed ominously ahead of Emily Blandish and Honoré Lechasseur, its glass and metal front throwing a dull light through the thick snow until it disappeared from view a few storeys up, eaten out of sight by the blizzard.

Lechasseur shivered deeper into his leather overcoat. 'Something tells me we're not back in Kansas,' he rumbled, a hint of America's South in his deep, soft voice.

The joke flew over Emily's head, as did so many of the cultural references she heard. She had no memories of her life beyond the most recent months she had spent in the company of Honoré and their exploits travelling through time. She was sure the memories were locked in her head somewhere, but for the moment they stayed infuriatingly out of reach. Most of the time, her amnesia wasn't that much of a problem and she got by without any difficulty, though she was aware that she did get odd looks when commenting that she had no idea who the Crazy Gang were or that she had never heard of Clark Gable. For a time it had bothered her, but now she was used to it, and this time she at least understood the gist of what Lechasseur had said – they weren't back in their own time period of 1950. When they had left on their previous jaunt through time, there had been no snow or gales forecast, and in 1950 at least, London had no buildings like the one in front of her. Whenever this was, it wasn't home. She shivered and looked round, searching for a clue as to where they had arrived. She caught brief glimpses of distant buildings as the snow momentarily lightened, but the blizzard mostly blocked them from sight, leaving the tower before them the only structure in full view. 'Shall we?' she asked.

Lechasseur let a few flakes settle on his hand and watched as the white snow melted to reveal his mocha-coloured skin. He hated snow. It was cold, wet and slippery, and something he'd had no experience of, growing up the humid climate of Louisiana. As a boy, he had heard of snow and thought it would be exciting and fun. He had been wrong. He loathed the stuff. 'Suits me,' he answered. 'Just get me indoors.'

They crunched their way forward, clutching each other's arms for support.

'These shoes weren't designed for this sort of weather,' Emily grumbled, more to herself than to Honoré. In front of the main doors, a curved glass overhang provided some respite from the wind, and Emily stamped her feet to loosen packed snow from her heels. 'We'll catch our deaths if we stay out here,' she said.

'I don't think we'll be much safer indoors,' Lechasseur answered, concern clear in his voice.

'Why?'

Emily followed the direction of Lechasseur's pointed finger. His reflection stared back at her, unease obvious on his face. Overprinted on his reflection was a familiar symbol, ornately engraved into the glass on one of the panels on the front of the building. Its lines were smoother than Emily recognised, and it looked as though it had been run through several committees and designers to give it a safer, more appealing appearance, but it was undeniably the same 'horned devil' symbol she had seen on their recent adventures in 1924 and 1892[1]. A shiver ran through Emily, and her legs went weak. There was something about that symbol.

A hint of a tail had been added, but the main image was unmistakable – a circular design with small, curved horns at the top.

Emily reached a hand towards the symbol but yanked it back abruptly as the glass panel slid aside. She looked sheepishly at Lechasseur, embarrassed at being so jumpy in front of her friend. 'An

1 See *Time Hunter: The Severed Man.*

automatic door,' she said, self-consciously.

'I guess,' Lechasseur nodded. 'So, do we go in?'

Squaring her shoulders, Emily took a deep breath and stepped through the door into the building.

'I'll take that as a yes,' Lechasseur muttered, and he followed Emily into the building's reception area. 'Why am I hearing the phrase, "Come into my parlour said the spider to the fly"?'

The glass door slid silently closed behind them.

CHAPTER ONE

- Where am I?
- Don't be afraid.
- Where am I?
- We won't hurt you.
- What is this place? Am I dead?
- We're not going to hurt you. Patience, would you talk to her?
- Very well, Joan. Please, be calm. No-one here will harm you.
- I can't see you.
- We will not hurt you, I promise you this. What is your name?
- Am I dead?
- What is your name?
- Alice. I'm Alice. Answer me. Am I dead? Am I?
- We do not know that, Alice.
- We might all be dead.

John Raymond carefully closed and locked his office. He straightened his tie and patted his hair into place. It was gone nine in the evening, and the building should be almost empty. He was unlikely to meet anyone, but if he did, he would look his best. He always liked to present a certain appearance – an appearance of affluence, of confidence. His suits were tailored by the most exclusive firms in London, and his haircuts cost more than an average person would earn in a week. They were all a part of letting the people he did business with know that John Raymond was a success. And success mattered to John Raymond.

Raymond's office was on the twentieth floor, at the very top of the building. Appropriate enough, given that he owned the tower. Officially, it was named the Dragon Industry Tower, but John Raymond had made sure that, even before it was built, everybody was calling it Raymond's Tower. This was his legacy, his great statement. A huge tower block built away from the centre of London. He was taking business back to the people. At least, that was the official line. The truth was that this land by the Thames on the site of an old dockyard was cheap and afforded space for parking. A commercial tower block like this one, filled with thriving businesses, would need hundreds of parking spaces.

But the tower wasn't filled with thriving businesses. Even when it had opened in a blaze of publicity eighteen months earlier, only half the available offices had been rented out. A year later, and the tower was less than a third full. Try as he might, Raymond hadn't been able to convince businesses to leave the hub of central London. The few that had had originally come had been tempted by the promise of reduced rent, and now more than half had given notice that they wouldn't be renewing their leases.

Raymond had made one significant miscalculation in building his tower. He had ensured that there would be ample parking spaces, but parking spaces were of little use if people couldn't get their cars to the car park. This section of London was served by a ring-road, which had been closed for major structural repairs four months before the tower opened, and was still closed now. The only alternative route was through winding, residential streets, which doubled the length of any journey. Businesses had sent representatives to look at the offices. They had made all the right, encouraging noises as Raymond had desperately wooed them with expensive dinners; but in the end, few had come. Raymond had lobbied the local council to delay the later stages of the road repairs. He had even offered bribes – some of them accepted. But the council had eventually stood by its decision. The roadworks continued.

Then, just to add to his problems, there were the persistent and, to

Raymond's mind, ridiculous stories of ghostly apparitions being encountered in the tower late at night. Raymond vaguely recalled hearing, when he had first bought the site, that there was a history of ghost stories attached to it, stretching right back to the Victorian era, and maybe beyond. There had even been someone offering ghost tours of the area to gullible foreign visitors. But Raymond had never expected that this would put businesses off from relocating to the tower. Admittedly, there had been that one time when he himself had thought that he had glimpsed the ghostly figure of a woman in a darkened office. That just went to show how powerful the human imagination could be, when fed with a diet of these ludicrous stories. Sadly, though, the few businesses he had managed to attract to the tower had found it increasingly difficult to recruit and retain security guards and cleaners to work in their offices after dark, increasing their reluctance to renew their leases, and damaging the tower's reputation still further.

For all his high-ranking friends, money and influence, there was nothing Raymond had been able to do to alter the situation. The tower was left half empty, and so it had become a huge drain on the rest of his empire. His great dream had become an albatross, pulling him towards bankruptcy. He had made discreet enquiries about selling the tower, but there were no buyers. He had dreamed that people would name the tower after him, and now they did. The press had dubbed it 'Raymond's Folly'. He had almost wept when he had seen that as the headline in *The Times*, running above the story detailing the collapse of his business empire. Raymond had contacted everyone he knew in business, called in every favour he could, and even some he had made up, but there was no way out. Within a month, probably less, he would be bankrupt and a laughing stock.

He walked the corridors slowly. As expected, the few offices that had been leased were now in darkness, the workers gone for the night. Raymond thought again of the ghost stories that had plagued the tower, and reflected that the place truly felt like a ghost ship. The atmosphere of failure was oppressive. Raymond made his way to the roof and took a deep breath of the cooler air. Rain was coming. He could see the clouds approaching along the Thames. In his life, John

Raymond had made a lot of enemies, and he knew how much they would revel in seeing him brought to his knees. They had called him arrogant, a rampant self-publicist, an ego-maniac. There was no denying that Raymond was a proud man. Too proud, certainly, to let his enemies see him reduced to a pauper by a court. He walked slowly to the edge of the roof and climbed up onto the safety wall that ran around the perimeter. He looked back at his building with pride. In time, it would be accepted as a success. He would be redeemed by history, but in his lifetime, John Raymond could never accept the tag of failure. Slowly and deliberately, he stepped off the side of his building.

Using a compact mirror, an attractive auburn-haired woman in her late thirties briskly applied make-up with a practised hand. Her schedule was hectic, and she didn't have time to waste hours in front of bathroom mirrors preening herself. Years of practice of re-touching between meetings meant that she could be done in moments. She glanced at the clock. Not bad. She would be on time. For once, work wouldn't delay her. She had just reached for her lipstick when she heard the first wail of a siren. A few seconds later, a second siren joined in the howling. She felt a terrible, sickening lurch in the pit of her stomach. The sirens were different in pitch – one was an ambulance and at least one of the others was the police. To be so loud they had to be coming here, to the tower, and somehow, in her heart, she knew something had happened to John.

• How can we all be dead if we're talking?
• We don't know, Alice.
• That's all you two say. We don't know. We don't know. We don't know. Do you know anything?
• Very little, I fear. Our circumstance is a mystery to Joan, me and all the other women in this place.
• Other women? How many of you … of us, are there?
• How many would you say, Patience?
• It is difficult to be precise. More than twenty, certainly, but fewer than thirty, I believe.

• You don't know that either.

• We cannot see each other.

• Patience is right, Alice. We can talk to each other only if we really want to. We have to try.

• And some of our number have withdrawn into themselves, preferring solitude, waiting alone in the darkness.

• Will it always be like this? I can't see anything but pitch black.

• In time you'll be able to … see us would be wrong. You sort of just know who's there, and you can see them in a way. Sense them.

• But we do not know how that comes to be, either. I believe that the Lord is protecting us.

• This can't be real. I don't believe in life after death. I don't believe in God.

• Are you a heretic?

• Don't be upset, Patience. Alice didn't mean to offend you. Did, you Alice?

• What? No. Look, if you're from the God-squad, I don't want to offend you. Right now, I'm wishing I had something to believe in.

• So few of us here have anything to believe in.

• God will provide, Joan.

• Sometimes, I don't believe either, Patience.

• What's that noise?

• It's nothing to be afraid of.

• So why do you sound so scared?

• It may pass.

• They're all terrified. I can hear them – all the people here. Make it stop.

• We cannot do that.

• It's coming this way. Patience?

• Joan! I am … I … dear Jesus in Heaven, guard this soul of your servant I ask you. I am …

• Patience?

• She's gone.

• She'll be back.

• How can you be sure?

• Because we always come back.

A thick layer of dust rested over what had once been a grand hall. A great wooden table, at least twenty-five feet long, filled half the length of the room. A heavy wooden chandelier hung over the table. Paintings adorned the walls: images of men ranging from the 15th Century through to Regency times. Their suits of armour, shields and swords decorated the hall. Years of dust and cobwebs covered them. The atmosphere was one of decay and neglect, of a once-majestic room ravaged by the unstoppable onslaught of passing time.

A dusty candle sitting in the centre of the table sparkled, and the wick flickered to life, apparently of its own volition. The flame took hold and cast a dancing yellow light around the room. As the shadows moved, other candles began sparking into life. On the great chandelier, all forty candles caught light at the same time, and as they did so, the dust on them faded. It wasn't burned off. It just melted into nothingness, as if it had never been there. The filth and grime that covered the room simply faded and disappeared, as if banished by the light. By the time the giant fireplace was filled with a roaring log-fire, the room was as it would have been in its pomp. The wood was scrubbed clean, the metals polished. Ornate, buffed wooden chairs were pushed in tight to the table, their back legs in two perfect rows on either side. Even the grimy, matted reeds that had covered parts of the stone floor had been replaced with fresh coverings. Twenty seconds earlier, it had been abandoned. Now, it was ready to welcome guests.

As quickly and as suddenly as the room had changed appearance, food began to appear on the table. Platters covered with roast chicken, boar and pheasant filled the centre of the table, surrounded by bowls and plates laden with fruits and vegetables. An open bottle of wine sat beside a pewter goblet, three quarters filled with the rich, red liquid, waiting.

A tormented scream broke the silence, and a young woman in her early twenties slowly appeared by the table. Her eyes were squeezed tightly shut and her hands clenched into fists. As she became completely solid, she lurched, as though out of practice at standing. Her eyes snapped open and she reflexively grabbed for the back of the nearest chair. She steadied herself and looked around. Her eyes widened. She was home. For a moment, she was shocked, and then relief flooded her face. She ran to the door and heaved at the handle.

The door refused to move. She pulled heavy curtains away from the windows. Beyond, there was only an inky blackness. She yanked the curtains closed again, as if not seeing the void outside would make it less real. She gripped the chair at the head of the table. Her chair. She felt an odd chill along her spine as she looked the length of the table at the empty chair facing hers. Despite everything that had happened, she wished that he was there with her. Nothing frightened him, especially in his own house. He would find a way to fight their way free. But he wasn't there. Despite the familiar faces looking down from two hundred years' worth of portraits, she was alone.

Hunger began to ache in the pit of her stomach. She hadn't eaten since … she had no idea. Time meant so little to her now. She fell on the food, tearing a leg from the roast chicken. The years her mother had spent teaching her the most proper table manners and the decorum a lady should show in public were forgotten as she bit and chewed as quickly as she could. She drained the wine from the goblet and filled it again, carelessly splashing the red liquid across the table as she did so. In time, she slowed, embarrassed by her lack of manners. Even though she was alone, her upbringing demanded the strictest standards. She ate more slowly, picking delicately at the food. As she ate, she thought. There had to be a way she could escape. She would find it. God would not abandon her to the fate she had faced. He would protect her and show her the way.

And then she heard the sound again. That awful noise. A sound like a demon tearing a scream from her soul. It was coming back for her.

'No.'

She ran to the door. Again it wouldn't move. A second door, leading to the kitchens, refused to open either. She looked around the room desperately. 'Please, God,' she pleaded. 'Protect me and save me from this thing. I am a good and honest Christian. Please, God, help me.'

Even as she prayed, the lights began to fade from the candles and the fire dimmed. Dust began to reappear over the furniture, and the reeds covering the floor darkened with age and became brittle. The food on the table became transparent and began to disappear.

She screamed, 'No! I won't go back!' But even as her words echoed round the hall, she faded away, leaving no trace that she had been there.

CHAPTER TWO

As soon as they entered the building, the warmth of the tower's heating embraced Emily and Lechasseur. 'Better?' Emily asked.

Lechasseur brushed the melting snow from his shoulder with his hat. 'Much. I think I can feel everything again.' He paused thoughtfully. 'Even the big toes are reporting in for duty.'

'Think yourself lucky you don't wear shoes like mine.' Emily shook more snow from her feet and looked ruefully at the low-heeled pumps. She'd be lucky if they weren't ruined. Actually, she thought, she was lucky that her ankles weren't ruined from trudging through snow in them – and shoes were easier to repair than ankles. She glanced over towards Honoré, who was standing by a display on one of the walls, reading the names on it. 'Do they give any clue about where we are?' she asked.

'Nope.' Lechasseur turned back to face Emily. 'Other than that the building is called the Dragon Industry Tower. And that it seems to be filled with the most boring sounding companies I ever heard of. Insurance, assurance, import, export.'

'Boring?' Emily tutted. 'I think the word you're looking for is *respectable*, Honoré.'

'Respectable?' Lechasseur nodded towards the symbol on the glass doors. 'With that on show?'

Emily's smile faded and she flicked a hand at two doors at the far end of the lobby. 'There, too,' she said. 'And there,' she added, indicating a subtle carving of the symbol cut into the front of the reception desk. Even with its polished, honed, corporate appearance, the horned symbol still brought a chill to Emily. She tried – and failed – to suppress a shiver. 'Perhaps not so respectable,' she said.

'Maybe things have changed,' Honoré offered. 'Or maybe it's just a coincidence' He sounded far from convincing – or convinced.

'Let's see what we can find here.' Emily moved around the reception desk and picked up a newspaper that lay face down on the desk. 'December, 1995,' she read. She gave the back page a cursory look, then handed the paper across to Honoré.

He scanned the front page briefly. Something about a movie named 'Goldeneye' ran in a banner along the top, with a handsome, dark-haired man looking grim while holding a gun. An actress with short reddish hair and wearing what was, to Lechasseur's eye, a very brief swimming costume, was leaning against him. 'Since when did a movie make front page news?' he muttered, then opened the first page of the paper. His lips pursed into a slightly wicked smile. 'Must be cold there, too.'

Emily peered over his shoulder. A topless blonde girl smiled out from page 3. 'So, in 1995, men are obsessed with women and football.'

'Well, that hasn't changed since 1950,' Lechasseur shrugged. 'And they still go to the movies.'

He looked around the reception area. A marble floor with a slightly differently coloured central aisle led to a set of four elevators. Corridors stretched off at right angles on either side of the elevators. The walls were decorated in light colours and highlighted with glass and shining metal. He didn't like it much. It was too sterile for his tastes. It felt like a designer had put it together to show how clever he was, without worrying about whether people would like working there or not. Or maybe this was just the way the fashion in architecture had changed since 1950. He remembered 2020 Tokyo, and the clinical design on show in that time. Either way, Lechasseur still didn't care for the place, though he noted with interest that Emily seemed completely at ease with the antiseptic surroundings.

The lights flickered, startling Lechasseur slightly. Emily didn't seem to have noticed him jump, though she did look a little uneasy as she turned to face him. 'It must be the weather disrupting the electricity,' she said.

'Must be,' Lechasseur agreed, adding another item to his list of reasons to hate snow.

'The wind's certainly strong enough. I can hear it in here.'

Lechasseur nodded. He hadn't noticed it before, but now that Emily mentioned the wind, he could make out a hollow, echoing sound just on the edge of his hearing.

'That's not right.' Emily's head was tilted to one side. 'It's getting closer.'

'Louder?' Lechasseur corrected.

Emily shook her head firmly. 'Closer,' she repeated.

'That doesn't make sense,' Lechasseur answered. 'Wind doesn't move like that.'

Emily's eyebrows shot up in irritation. 'I know that,' she responded, a little more snippily than she had intended. 'But how does it sound to you?'

Honoré concentrated on the sound. Emily was right. 'It *does* sound like it's getting closer,' he conceded. For a second, he was reminded of the sound of German artillery as it had whistled through the air, getting louder as it came closer, before it detonated and the screams started.

Emily pointed along the corridor to the left of the lifts. 'I think it's coming from this direction,' she said, and without waiting for Lechasseur, she strode off.

'What do you expect to find?' Lechasseur called, running a few steps to catch up with Emily.

'I'm not sure,' Emily answered. She chuckled wryly. 'Probably an open window with the wind whistling through it.'

'Sounds good to me.'

'Of course, it's far more likely to be something hideous and terrifying, ready to bite our heads off.'

Lechasseur glowered. 'You had to go and spoil it.'

'You're not nervous, are you, Honoré?' Emily smiled.

'Why don't we just keep looking for this open window of …' He stopped abruptly, and the smile on Emily's lips died. The sound they had thought was the wind had become clearer and far more distinct – and unmistakably a woman's scream. A long, almost impossibly drawn-out scream, that finally and abruptly cut off.

Emily grasped a door-handle. 'She's through here.' She twisted the handle, but the door stayed resolutely closed. 'Locked.'

'Let me try,' Lechasseur said, moving past Emily and leaning his weight on the door.

The scream sounded again, this time even closer, and the fear was obvious. 'Try again,' Emily said urgently.

'I'm trying.' Lechasseur barged his shoulder against the door as he turned the handle. Again nothing happened.

''Ere, what the hell are you lot doing there!'

Emily and Lechasseur spun round. Approaching them at speed from the corridor on the far side of the lifts was an elderly man in a uniform that appeared to have been designed for someone much younger – flashy epaulettes, shiny buttons, a gaudy red stripe down the sides of the trousers and a carefully-designed but painfully tacky logo reading '5-Star Security'. To his credit, the guard – whose name, Dorkins, was displayed on a tag pinned to his breast pocket – carried the uniform with better grace than it deserved.

Lechasseur, realising that it must appear as if he and Emily had been trying to break into the office, attempted to rescue the situation: 'Erm, this isn't what it looks like. You see, we heard a woman screaming and …' He broke off his feeble explanation as he realised that Dorkins was no longer listening to him, but was now staring over his and Emily's shoulders at the locked door behind them, an expression of mounting terror on his face.

Lechasseur and Emily both turned to see what had seized Dorkins' attention. To their utter astonishment, the spectral figure of a young woman in Regency clothing was passing straight through the door and looming towards them along the dimly-lit corridor. Instinctively, they ducked, while the terror-stricken Dorkins flung himself to the floor.

Honoré threw his hand across his face for protection. As the figure passed, the trailing cuff of her sleeve passed through him. There was no pain from the contact, only an icy chill, as if she had drained all the heat from his body as she passed. 'What was that?' he gasped.

'I'm no expert,' Emily said quietly, 'but I'd say it looked like a ghost.'

'I hoped it was just me.'

Ignoring Dorkins' feeble protests, Emily and Lechasseur hurried after the pale figure. The ghost stopped suddenly and spun towards them. Her mouth was open in a silent scream; her face filled with terror. She stretched out her hands towards them, pleading. She slipped by them and rose higher, her form fading as it ascended through the ceiling.

'I never believed in ghosts,' Lechasseur said quietly.

'I don't know if she was a ghost or not,' Emily answered. 'But did you see the expression on her face?'

Lechasseur nodded. 'Terrified. But so would I be if I was ... whatever she is.'

'She went through the ceiling. Do you think we should follow her?'

'Are you seriously asking me that? Personally, I'd rather turn myself in to that security guard.'

'Honoré.'

'All right,' Lechasseur grumbled. 'We ought to follow her. You're right.'

Emily pressed the button for the lift, carefully avoiding looking at the horned symbol. 'Aren't I always?'

'Can I plead the Fifth on that?'

A bell chimed, and the lift door slid silently open. 'Saved by the bell.' Emily stepped into the lift and Honoré followed. 'Where to?'

Lechasseur hit the button for the top floor. 'Where else for classy folks like us?'

CHAPTER THREE

'Not bad.' Lechasseur took in the lift's interior. Ornately decorated panels featuring a fire-breathing dragon – representing Dragon Industry, he assumed, and far more welcoming than the company's logo – reached almost halfway to the ceiling. Heavily polished mirrors filled the top half of the walls. The interiors of the doors featured two dragons posed so that when the doors slid shut, battle was joined.

The lift gave a slight lurch as it reached the top floor. There was a subdued chime and the doors slid open. Emily and Honoré moved out onto the landing. They had two choices. To their left there was a pair of doors marked *Giovanni Imports*; to the right, the plaque on the doors read *Christopher and Jones, Financial Services*.

'Do you have a preference?' Emily asked.

Lechasseur grimaced. 'Never much cared for titles like Financial Services,' he said. 'Too much like a loan shark trying to sound legit.'

'So it's the import business for us?' Emily reached for the doors and they swung inwards easily. 'Unlocked,' she said. 'Lucky for us.' She pushed the doors wide open to reveal a set of offices decorated in warm, friendly colours. They stepped through the doors ...

... into nothingness.

Faster than their eyes could register, the offices disappeared and they were standing – *floating?* – in a jet black void.

'Emily?'

'I'm all right. Did you see what happened?'

Lechasseur looked round quickly, trying not to show any panic. 'It was too fast for me,' he said. 'Can you see anything at all?'

'No.' Emily grasped at the air around them.

'Hopefully, you're going to tell me the lights just went out.'

'If they did, why can we still see each other?' Emily hunkered down and wafted her hand through the space where a floor should have been. She ran her hand under both their pairs of feet without encountering any obstruction. 'And we don't seem to be standing on anything, either.'

Lechasseur laughed uncomfortably. 'You know, if this was a Bugs Bunny cartoon, this'd be the time we'd fall.'

He took a deep breath and looked around again. The view hadn't changed – still pitch black all around them – but he forced some confidence into his voice. 'Okay, I guess we have to find a way out of here.'

'At a wild guess,' Emily said thoughtfully, 'I'd say we take that door?'

'Door?'

Some way ahead of them – they could only guess at the actual distance – a door had appeared. A regular, wooden door, like the front door of a house, painted a reassuring blue. 'I'll be …' Honoré breathed.

'I think it's getting closer.'

Sure enough, the door was growing larger, the panels becoming clearer, the handle and letterbox growing more distinct.

'Are we getting closer to the door or is it coming closer to us?'

'Or both?' Emily offered.

The door stopped a few inches from where they stood, entirely incongruous in the void surrounding them.

Emily ran a finger gingerly around the letter box. 'It's solid enough.'

Lechasseur rapped his knuckles on the door. The sound was reassuringly wooden. He was surprised by the lack of an echo. For some reason, he had expected the sound to reverberate.

'Are you expecting an answer?' Emily asked. 'A butler telling us we're expected and asking if we would care to have some tea?'

'If somebody puts a door in the middle of, well, wherever this is, my guess is that they want us to go through.'

'Obviously,' Emily answered, testily. 'And I imagine there's only one way to find out what's waiting inside.'

'We look through the letterbox?' Lechasseur suggested, hopefully.

Emily twisted at the handle and pushed the door open. Without waiting to see what lay through the door, she stepped across the threshold.

'Wait!' Lechasseur threw up a hand to stop her. Too late. 'I really wish you hadn't done that,' he grumbled, and then, for the second time in an hour, Honoré Lechasseur followed Emily through a door into the unknown.

• It's all right, Patience. Patience.
• No! No, I can't be here again, Joan. I won't be!
• What happened to her?
• I can't be back here.
• Patience, you're safe here. You know you're safe.
• What happened? Where did she go?
• Is she all right, miss?
• Go away, Mary.
• Did you go home, milady?
• Leave me alone.
• I just want to know …
• Go away!
• Joan, what's happening?
• Alice. Take Mary away from here.
• How do I do that?
• You'll find out. You just do.
• But …
• No buts, Mary. Go with Alice.
• Yes, miss.
• Patience? Patience?
• I thought I was free, Joan.
• You're safe enough, Patience.
• I don't want to be here. I can't bear it.
• Your name's Mary, isn't it?
• Yes, miss.

- Alice. Call me Alice.
- Oh, I couldn't do that.
- Why not?
- Well, it wouldn't be proper.
- Of course it would. It's my name.
- No, I couldn't. The mistress would never stand for it.
- Why?
- I'm only a servant. I shouldn't talk to the likes of you. Not so familiar.
- Your mistress? You work for Patience?
- Yes, miss. Well, sort of.
- What do you mean 'sort of'? You do or you don't, surely.
- I shouldn't have interrupted.
- Where are you going? No. Stop.
- I shouldn't stay. I'm sorry, miss.
- Don't … Stop! Where's she gone? Hello? Mary? She's gone. Joan, she's gone … Joan? Joan? Hello? Joan? Patience? Where are you? Where have you all gone?

Lechasseur stepped through the door into the last thing he expected – an utterly normal house. The surroundings startled him for a moment, and he simply stood in the hall, looking round at the peeling, dull wallpaper, the faded pictures on the walls and the worn but well-tended old furniture. Apart from the thick coating of dust that layered everything for the entire length of the hall, Lechasseur could have been in any one of a dozen houses he knew in London. Actually, a few of those houses weren't far short of being as dusty as this place. Not all of Lechasseur's associates had time to be houseproud.

Emily was drawing a spiral in the dust on a small table with her finger. 'It's not what you expected, is it?' she asked.

'No,' Lechasseur admitted. 'But then, I don't know exactly what I did expect.'

Emily inspected the dust on the end of her finger. 'Nor me. This dust seems real.'

'So?'

'I don't know.' Emily blew the dust from her finger. 'The tower was in 1995, yes?'

'According to the newspaper in the lobby,' Lechasseur confirmed.

Emily picked up some letters that were lying on the table, and blew the dust from them. She squinted at the envelopes. 'I can't quite make out the postmark on these.' She passed two of them across to Honoré. 'You take a look.'

Lechasseur tilted and angled the letters into the light, trying to find some part of the postmark left visible. 'If there was a mark, it's long gone.'

'In that case, I don't see much choice.' She slipped her fingers into one of the envelopes and plucked out a letter.

'Hey!' Lechasseur protested. 'We can't just read somebody's mail like that.'

'Why not?' Emily asked blandly. 'We need to know where we are. So far, these letters are our best chance of finding out.'

'But they're private.'

'I know.' She ran her finger in the dust again and showed the grime to Lechasseur. 'But I think whoever was here left a long time ago.'

'Maybe you're right,' Lechasseur conceded. 'But it still feels wrong.'

'Suddenly, I think you're right.' Emily put down the envelope she had opened.

'What is it?'

'Read for yourself.' Emily handed the letter across.

The message was hand-written on headed Army notepaper.

Dear Mrs Barton,

It is with regret that I must inform you of your son George's death in battle here in France. He was a fine soldier and a fine young man, who died in a brave action defending his comrades and taking an enemy position. In every way he was a credit to his family and to his country. I trust you will find solace in the knowledge that your son gave his life in a just cause. I assure you that his sacrifice will not be a vain one.

Yours sincerely,
Colonel Richard Stewart

'It's not much of a way to tell someone that her child has died,' Emily said sadly.

Lechasseur carefully folded the letter and replaced it in the envelope. 'By the end of the War, there were so many letters being sent home that most commanding officers didn't have time to write to the families of the dead. That letter might have been short, but at least this Colonel Stewart took the time to write. Mrs Barton would also have gotten an official telegram from the War Office telling her that her son was dead. This kind of letter was to let the family know that the death mattered and wasn't for nothing.'

'You might be right.' From Emily's tone, it was clear that she was unconvinced.

'November 1944,' Lechasseur mused, looking at the date at the top of the letter. 'There was a big push back then. I read about it in the newspapers. Colonel Stewart must have written this on the march. I wonder how many he had to write?' Lechasseur set the letter back on the table. 'I heard of a captain who cried every time he wrote one of those letters. Can't say I blame him.'

'Did you ever have to write one?'

Lechasseur shook his head. 'I wasn't an officer, Emily.'

'This is the letter from the authorities telling her that her son was dead.' Emily was holding a thin sheet of almost transparent paper. The message on it was brief and to the point. 'It's so cold and impersonal. He's dead, we're sorry. I can see why the officer would want to write to the families.'

Lechasseur shook himself. This was bringing back too many memories. 'Okay,' he said. 'We were in 1995, now we're around '44 or '45.'

'Are we?' Emily asked. She was running her finger along a wooden panel inset into the wall. Her finger carefully followed the grain of the wood.

'From the way you said that, I'm guessing we're not.'

Emily turned. 'There's something about this house.' She tilted her head, and her eyebrows knitted in concentration. 'I'm not sure what it is, but it's something to do with time.'

Lechasseur smiled. 'I kind of guessed time was involved.'

'No,' Emily snapped, more sharply than she intended. 'I mean here, in this place.' She looked around the hall, as if she hoped the answer would become obvious to her. 'I don't know how to explain it. There's something wrong with the way this house relates to time. Can't you feel it? Time is at odds with every inch of this house.'

Lechasseur tried to relax and let his mind reach out for whatever Emily was sensing. Other than a general feeling of unease, nothing registered. 'Sorry,' he said. 'I don't feel it.'

'Time is wrong here,' Emily said slowly. 'I don't know how else to explain it.'

'That makes me feel better,' Lechasseur said wryly.

'Perhaps if we had better light in here, we'd feel less nervous.' Emily flipped the bakelite switch by the door up and down a few times. The lights stayed off.

'Did you expect them to work?' Lechasseur asked.

'It was worth trying.'

'Not really.' Lechasseur looked more closely at the light on the wall, and then tapped the light switch. 'Some of these houses were converted for electricity before the War, but hadn't started using it, even by 1950.' He struck a match and turned a small knob on the light. There was a faint hissing sound before the gas lit and a dull, yellowish light flickered and brightened the hall. 'It's not electricity, but it's better than nothing.'

Emily looked unconvinced. 'I'd still rather have electricity.'

'I'd rather be on a beach with Dorothy Lamour,' Lechasseur shrugged, 'but here I am.'

'The gas will have to do, I suppose,' Emily conceded. 'Since we're here – wherever here really is – we probably should look around.'

'Seems fair.'

Two doors led from the left side of the hallway. On the right side, a flight of stairs ascended to a murky upstairs. A door directly under the stairs led, no doubt, to a cupboard, and there was another door further back on the same wall. A fifth door was at the end of the hall. It seemed more solid than the others. The back door, most likely. 'Any preferences?' Lechasseur asked.

'Not really,' Emily replied. The bottom stair creaked as she stepped on it, making Lechasseur's head snap round. 'Nervous?' she asked.

'What do you think?' Lechasseur grumbled.

'I …' A flashing movement caught the corner of Emily's eye, and she swung her head to the head of the stairs. 'Hello?'

'You see something?' Lechasseur asked.

Emily nodded. 'I think so. Just for a second. It looked like a boy, wearing black trousers. They looked too short for him.'

The darkness hung ominously above the stairs. 'I don't see anybody there now,' Lechasseur said thoughtfully.

'Perhaps we frightened him,' Emily offered. She began moving slowly up the stairs. 'Hello?' she said again. 'My name's Emily. Are you there?' She stopped abruptly. 'Oh.'

'What is it?' Lechasseur hurried up the steps to join her.

'I don't think it's dark upstairs,' Emily said. She raised her hand towards the darkness, but instead of disappearing into shadows, her hand stopped at its edge. 'The darkness is solid,' she grunted, pushing against an unyielding wall of blackness.

Lechasseur added his strength to Emily's, heaving against the invisible barrier. 'Okay,' he conceded. 'I guess we're not getting to see upstairs.'

'I wonder if there is an upstairs?' Emily murmured to herself. 'If not, where did the boy go?'

'Are you sure you saw him?' Lechasseur asked. 'You're certain it wasn't a reflection or a shadow or something?'

'You think I imagined him?' Emily asked sharply. 'And I don't remember ever seeing shadows wearing hand-me-down britches before.'

'Are you sure it's a boy?' asked Honoré. 'Remember that thing in 1950, which just looked like a boy?[2]'

'I'm not sure. It was only a fleeting glimpse.'

'Well, whatever it was, it's not there now.' Lechasseur headed back downstairs. 'Why don't we see what we can find down here?' he called back.

Emily looked deeply into the darkness for a moment, then followed Honoré. 'All right,' she said. 'We might as well try these doors.'

The handle on the nearest door turned, but the door stayed

2 See *Time Hunter: The Severed Man.*

resolutely closed. Lechasseur rattled it again. Still no movement.

'Locked?' Emily offered.

'Jammed, anyway,' Lechasseur answered. 'I guess this would be the front room.'

'There's another room on this side of the house,' Emily said. 'Perhaps there's a door from that into the front room.'

'It's worth a try.'

They made their way to the other door on the left side of the hallway. Framed family photographs were proudly displayed at regular intervals along the wall. On another small table, the remains of a bunch of flowers hung black and withered to twigs, covered with dust. Emily wiped the table with a finger. The wood gleamed underneath. Whatever had happened to this house, it had once been looked after with pride. Emily began to feel a great sadness for the woman who had lived in the house. She had loved her family – she assumed that a middle-aged uniformed man in a number of the photographs was the father, Mr Barton, rather than the son – and had tended her home with great care. Had the news of her son's death proved too much for her to deal with? Certainly something had made this houseproud woman abandon her home without even taking her letters with her. Oddly, even though she had never met the woman, Emily felt an empathy for Mrs Barton, and a sadness, too, as she felt a wave of certainty that whatever had happened in this house, there hadn't been a happy outcome for Mrs Barton. The realisation made Emily's shoulders sink, and a sigh escaped her. She felt weary, as if this certainty about Mrs Barton's fate had knocked the energy from her.

'Emily?' Lechasseur asked, concern clear in his voice. 'Are you all right?'

Emily shook herself. Becoming maudlin would do no-one any good. 'Fine,' she answered briskly. She reached for the handle. Lechasseur caught her hand.

'Before we go in, maybe we should try the back door.'

'In case there's a way out to …?'

'Who knows?' Lechasseur tugged the handle and pushed the door open. The black void sat outside, stretching out into eternity. 'Worth a try.' Lechasseur shrugged. He pulled the door shut. 'We're not leaving that way. I guess it was too much to hope for.'

'What was that?' Emily asked.

'I said …'

'No,' Emily interrupted. 'I'm sure I heard someone.'

Lechasseur looked around with suspicion. 'Saying what?'

'I don't know. It was like the echo of a whisper.' She looked wryly at her friend. 'That's not much help, is it?'

'No,' Lechasseur admitted. 'But I don't think you're imagining it, either. Everything about this house is wrong.'

'It's …' Emily stopped and shook herself. 'Listen to us,' she scolded. 'We sound like a pair of children frightened by a ghost story.' Firmly, she twisted the handle of the second door in the left-hand wall. It swung open to reveal a small back room dominated by a sturdy old wooden table. A matching chair sat on each side of the table, with two odd chairs pushed back against the wall on either side of a heavy-looking sideboard. A heavy bakelite wireless had pride of place on the adjacent wall, with one worn but comfortable-looking armchair close by. More framed pictures were prominent on the sideboard and the walls. Mrs. Barton's pride in her family shone in this room as well.

Emily lifted one photograph. A stiffly-posed family looked back at her. The middle-aged soldier from the photographs in the hall stood rigidly to attention beside a seated, matronly woman of around forty. Seven children – six girls and a single boy – surrounded them. For all the stiffness of the pose, the affection within the family group was obvious. One of the elder girls held a younger sister's hand. The father's hand rested on his son's shoulder, his other hand touching his wife's arm, her hand closed over his. Emily carefully set the photograph back in place. The rest of the photographs were all of the family. She smiled a little and wondered briefly if she had ever been a part of a family like this one. She started and spun round as a click came from behind her.

Lechasseur had turned on the wireless set and was turning the volume up. 'It'll take a while to warm up,' he said. 'These sets don't work cold.'

'Do you expect to hear anything?'

The hiss of static began to come from the front of the wireless. 'Only that.' Lechasseur turned the tuning dial back and forth, searching for a signal. The hiss remained constant. 'No interference, none of the usual noises you get when you're tuning a wireless.' He turned the dial and the set clicked off. 'There's no signal for it to pick up.' He stood and looked at the opposite wall, which he had hoped would lead to the front room. 'No door to the front room, either.'

'Is that usual?' Emily wondered. 'It would make sense for there to be a way through, wouldn't you think?'

Lechasseur shrugged uncertainly. 'I'm not sure. But I've heard that some people keep their front room for special occasions. They don't use it except when they've got guests.'

'Do we count as guests, do you think?' Emily tapped on the wall. It felt – and sounded – disappointingly solid.

Lechasseur joined her. 'The question is, if we are guests, are we welcome or unwelcome ones?'

'If we could be brought here, presumably we could just as easily have been killed,' Emily reasoned.

'That's a cheerful thought.'

Ignoring the interruption, Emily continued. 'So, we can assume that we're not in any immediate danger.'

'That's a big assumption,' Lechasseur countered. 'Especially when it's been made clear that we're not going anywhere in a hurry.'

'Then perhaps it would make sense to explore the places we can go?' Emily offered. She glanced briefly at the photographs decorating the sideboard. 'I want to know what happened here, Honoré.'

Something in Emily's tone caught Lechasseur's attention. He wasn't certain if it was simply the bizarre situation niggling at his friend's nerves or if she was feeling a personal link of some kind. She certainly seemed to have some empathy for this Mrs Barton, though Lechasseur conceded that it would be hard not to feel for the woman. He wondered what was affecting Emily, but decided against asking outright. He knew better than to pry with Emily. She could be defensive and snippy when she felt her privacy was being invaded. If it was important, she would tell him, in time. And if she didn't? Well, Lechasseur had talked more stubborn people than Emily Blandish into giving him answers before. Though he had to admit, there weren't that many who could be more stubborn than Emily when she set her mind to something.

Lechasseur headed back out into the hall. 'So, which of the places we are allowed to go do you think we should try first?'

The two doors set in the wall facing the room they were leaving seemed the obvious choices. 'You try one, I'll try the other,' Emily said, and reached for the nearest door-handle. 'I imagine this one is the kitchen. You can have the cupboard under the stairs.'

'Thanks,' Lechasseur drawled sourly. 'I notice you don't take the one that's probably dark and full of spiders.'

'Don't worry,' Emily smiled. 'If you see any spiders, just scream and I'll come and deal with them for you.'

'Funny girl,' Lechasseur muttered. 'You should be on the stage. Then you'd be used to big, empty houses.'

'I heard that,' said Emily, and poked her tongue out at him.

'You were meant to,' Honoré said. He opened his door and peered in. Instead of the small, confined space of a cupboard, he found the head of a set of stairs that led down into darkness. 'There are stairs here,' he said. Emily didn't reply. 'I said, there are stairs here,' he repeated, louder this time. Again, Emily didn't respond. He turned towards his friend, just in time to see the kitchen door click shut.

CHAPTER FOUR

- Hello? Mary? Where have you gone? Mary? Patience? Joan?
- They're not far away.
- Mary? No. You're not Mary.
- Nah. I'm not that poor cow.
- So who are you?
- You're new, aren't ya?
- Is it obvious?
- You can't hide much here for long.
- I'm Alice Monroe. Who are you?
- Tess.
- That's it? Just Tess?
- What do you need to know anything else for?
- I just thought …
- Well, don't. Best thing you can do here is not think.
- How can you not think?
- You do. After a while, you just do. If you start thinking about where you were before, well, that don't do you no good.
- Why?
- And don't think about getting out of here, neither.
- If we got here, there must be a way out.
- What do you know about it? You just got here.
- I know the laws of science. If we can be brought here, then there has

to be a way we can get out.
- Oh, we can get out.
- You see?
- But we always get brought back.
- How? Is that what happened to Patience?
- The snooty cow was the one it took, then?
- Patience.
- Patience? That's a laugh.
- Why?
- 'Cause that's all we have left here. Patience.
- How long have you been here?
- Dunno.
- Think.
- Don't tell me what to do. There's enough pushy cows here already.
- I'm sorry. I didn't mean to push you around, Tess. But can you remember how long you've been here?
- No. But it's been a long time. Ever such a long time.
- Who's Prime Minister? Do you know that?
- What would the likes of me care about summat like that?
- You're young. You can't be more than, what? Fifteen? Sixteen.
- I'm over sixteen and a half. Nearer seventeen, if you please.
- Then you must have seen the Prime Minister on TV. You can't have spent all day watching MTV.
- What are you talking about? Was you at the poppy before you was taken? What are you talking about? What the 'ell's MTV?
- You don't know what MTV is?
- No. But I'm not stupid, so you can take that out of your voice.
- What about school? Didn't you study politics at school?
- I ain't never been to no school.
- That doesn't make sense.
- You're the one as is makin' no sense. School's not for my kind.
- What kind is that?
- The poor. I had to work. I didn't have no time to waste at school. You're off your head.
- What year is it? Who's on the throne?
- I dunno now.

• When you came here. What was the year and who was on the throne.
• 1892, and Queen Vic was queen. I saw her once, an' all. Went up West, special. Right sour-faced old cow, she was. Face like misery, she had. A waste of a day, that was.
• 1892?
• That's what I said.
• It can't be.
• It's a fact.
• But I was born in 1959. I was in 1995 when I was brought here.
• Yeah.
• That doesn't surprise you?
• Everybody here is from somewhere different in time.
• But that's impossible.
• It's true, hon.
• Who said …? Wait. I can sense you.
• That's Sandi, that is.
• Tess is right. We're all from different times. And if you're going to say 'That's impossible' again, don't. It's a real drag. I heard it a million times since I got here.
• When was that?
• You say you're from, what? '95? Twenty-six years, hon. Who'd have thought twenty-six years in Hell would be so damn dull?
• What do you mean, Hell?
• Isn't it obvious, hon?
• Hell?
• Where else should we be? We're all dead. In Hell, where we deserve.

'Emily?' Lechasseur rattled the kitchen door-handle again, but the door remained stubbornly shut. Abandoning the handle, he braced himself against the facing wall and kicked hard at the door itself, his foot driving at its central panel with all the strength he could muster. He knew these old houses. He knew how they were put together. The door should have been sent splintering into the kitchen. At the very least, the bolt-mechanism of the handle should have broken, letting the door open. Instead, the door stayed resolutely closed, and Lechasseur's foot felt like he had just tried to kick his way through the wall of St Paul's. He kicked the door again, even though he knew it would be futile. It hadn't moved an inch. Lechasseur swore under his breath. What should he do? Wait here for Emily or continue his own exploration?

'Emily,' he called. 'If you can hear me, I'm going to take a look down those stairs. See if maybe I can find a way up to you.' As Lechasseur had expected, there was no answer. He called again, saying that he would be back within a few minutes. He was certain Emily hadn't heard his call. At the head of the basement stairs, Lechasseur took half a step, then stopped. He returned to the hall, pulled the nearer of the two tables to the doorway and wedged it there, so that it would stop the cellar door from closing behind him. He had taken half a dozen steps down and was reaching in his pocket for his lighter when he heard the door bang against the table.

Emily turned sharply as she heard the kitchen door slam shut behind her. She sighed as the door rebounded open instantly, revealing the hall outside. 'I'm all right,' she called. 'Don't worry about me.' There was no answer. 'No, really,' she added sarcastically. 'I'm absolutely fine.' Still no answer. Emily shook her head fondly. Honoré was probably exploring the cellar already and hadn't even heard the kitchen door banging. She returned her attention to the kitchen. For a moment, Emily couldn't quite work out what was wrong with the room, and then it struck her. It was clean. Unlike the rest of the house, it was free from years of dust and inattention. It was spotlessly clean, exactly as Emily imagined Mrs Barton would have kept it. The kitchen table was scrubbed, the cooker gleamed and crockery was stacked neatly waiting to be put away. And there was a smell, too. A warm, comforting smell, as though something had recently been cooked. Emily passed her hand by the front of the cooker and yanked it back immediately. The oven was still hot. A large kettle, sitting on the back hob, began to whistle and steam. Emily reached for a cloth hanging from a hook by the cooker and moved the kettle from the hob. But the kettle's whistling grew louder. Emily peered at it in confusion for a second, until she realised that the whistling was actually coming from outside. She had a fraction of a second to realise what was happening, what was causing the whistling, before the house exploded around her. The blast sent her sprawling onto the floor, shattered glass and broken masonry flying around her, dust filling the air, choking her as grit and debris clogged her throat. She squeezed her eyes tightly shut to keep the grime and smoke from stinging her eyes. From nearby, she heard the sound of footsteps and the hollow clunking of broken bricks moving against one another. She opened her eyes tentatively. 'Honoré?'

She wasn't inside the house any longer. Instead, she was lying outside on a huge pile of rubble; all that remained of the house. The footsteps belonged to a fireman, looking at the devastation with horror in his face. Emily followed his gaze and saw a small, still hand sticking through the rubble, its skin charred and scorched till it was almost black. Emily closed her eyes to blot out the horror of the sight. Even before she opened her eyes, she knew that she had moved again. The sharp, bumpy carpet of bricks had been replaced by smooth, even, cool linoleum. She was back in the kitchen. The undamaged kitchen from before the bomb had torn it apart. The kettle still bubbled contentedly, the whistling sound dying as the water cooled slightly. The kitchen looked exactly as it had, but the comforting atmosphere had gone. In its place, Emily felt an apprehensive chill.

She moved hurriedly back out into the hall.

'Honoré?' she called. 'Honoré?' As she had anticipated, only silence answered. The dust and grime were gone and the hallway shone, every surface freshly polished, every picture frame straight and evenly lined up on the wall or on the tables. The letters that had so affected Emily a few minutes earlier were nowhere to be seen. Emily felt her unease about the house's relationship with time growing stronger, as if time itself was pushing against the walls. Resisting an initial urge to block out the sensations, Emily forced herself to relax. She closed her eyes, eased her mind open and reached out mentally, trying to find the source of these sensations. A coldness enveloped her and rapidly grew more intense. She began to feel the time that surrounded her. It should have been moving, flowing as the universe intended it to. Instead, time was held here. At least, small snatches of it were. Tiny fragments of time held captive and straining to be set free. Time itself was …

Click.

Emily's eyes snapped open. There had been a sound in the house. Quiet, almost imperceptible, but definitely there. A single click.

After a short period of silence, Emily heard the static hiss and whine of a wireless set being tuned.

• What do you mean, we're dead? We can't be dead. We're talking.
• Look around you, hon. Try to touch something. Try to touch me.
• I can't.
• Of course you can't. You can't touch dead people.
• I'm not dead. I can't be. Tess?
• I dunno what this place is.
• But you don't think it's Hell.
• I ... I dunno.
• Listen, hon. No disrespect to Little Tess, but she spent most of her time whacked out of her skull on a mixture of gin and opium. She wouldn't know if a bus ran over her feet.
• Hey. I'm not stupid.
• I didn't say you were, hon.
• I might not know smart words like you, but I'm not stupid.
• Ignore her, Tess. Tell me, where do *you* think we are?
• I told you. I don't know.
• You must have some idea.
• You're wasting your time with her, hon.
• Be quiet, Sandi. Tess, you must have thought about it. You said you'd been here for ages.
• Yeah.
• So you must have thought about where this is.
• Well, I have sort of thought of something.
• Go on.
• It's the last place I remember being before I was here.
• Where?
• A little place I goes sometimes, when I got the cash. Chang Wu's. He's a Chinee. Got some real good stuff, he has.
• Stuff? What kind of stuff?
• What kind of stuff do you think? I told you. He's a Chinee. What else would they have? I go there to chase the dragon.

• Dragon? Opium? You were in an opium den?

• Yeah. The law don't bother the place – except when they're in for some themselves. Chang Wu's got the best stuff, too. Says his brother brings it in on the boats.

• Lucky you, hon. I'd kill for some grass about now.

• Go on, Tess.

• I was there. He'd give me a real nice spot. All quiet and out of the way. He said I could chase the dragon all night if I wanted. He's all right for a foreigner. Always dead polite, and he never tried nothing on with me.

• Not that you remember. Maybe while you were off chasing he was copping a feel.

• He wouldn't.

• Ignore her, Tess. How were you having the opium?

• A sort of pipe thing. You just puff on it and you're away.

• I know the thing.

• Do you?

• No, I don't do it myself. I've seen them around, though. Bongs, we call them in my day. Some shops sell them as conversation pieces. Charge a fortune for them, too.

• One minute I was there, the next I'm here.

• That sounds familiar, if you substitute my office for your … whatever you'd call it. Drug den? So, suddenly you're here.

• Yeah. And that's why I think I know where this is.

• Tell me?

• My head.

• What?

• This is my head. Everybody knows you have really weird dreams when you mix gin with the poppy. That's what I'm doing. I'm dreaming it all.

• She thinks she's tripping and we're part of her trip.

• That's absurd.

• Amen to that.

• But I don't believe this is Hell either. I don't believe in Hell – or Heaven.

• Give it time, hon, and you will.

• Stop calling me hon! I'm not your bloody hon, okay?

• Whatever you say.

• Your idea that we're in Hell is just as stupid as her thinking we're in some sort of spaced out trip.

• Don't call me stupid. I hate that. I'm not stupid. I'm not.

• Of course you're not, Tess, dear.

• Joan?

• Yes, Alice. Now, Tess, nobody thinks you're stupid.

• She does. She said so.

• She's new here, Tess. She's upset and confused. And sometimes we all say things we don't mean.

• I don't believe I'm part of her trip.

• Trip? I don't understand, Alice.

• Trip. Hallucination. Brought on by drugs.

• No, I'm afraid we're all here. Alice, where's Mary?

• I don't know. She got upset and sort of, well, just disappeared.

• She does that sometimes. It's easy to lose yourself here.

• Her head's not all it should be anyway, poor cow.

• Tess! Please don't use that horrible word.

• Sorry, Joan. I'll try not to use it.

• Thank you.

• At least when you can hear me.

• Cheeky young devil.

• How's her ladyship?

• Patience? She's upset, as you'd imagine. But we all are, when it happens.

• When what happens?

• There's so much you'll have to get used to, Alice. So much we'll have to prepare you for.

• I don't understand any of this.

• None of us does, dear. Like Tess and Sandi, we all come up with ideas.

• All I want is some answers.

• Answers are the one thing we can't give you, Alice. We don't have any.

• What about Patience? You must be able to tell me what happened to her.

• Ain't just her it happens to. Happens to us all, some time or other.

• But we won't have to think about that for a while yet, Tess.

• Why not?

• Cos someone was took not long ago, and there's always a good gap between times.

• This isn't making any sense. Maybe this is a dream – only it's me who's dreaming it.

• I'll explain as much as I can.

• Joan …

• Tess can help.

• It's not that, Joan. It's coming back.

• Nonsense. It can't be. Patience was only just brought back.

• I know it don't make sense, but it's coming. I can feel it.

• You know, I hate agreeing with the little goof, but I think she's right.

• Sandi? I'd almost forgotten you were here.

• They're right, Joan. I can feel something. It's like …

• A cold wind.

• It's like all the hairs on the back of my neck are standing on end, except …

• Except we don't have no hairs or necks here.

• You're right, Tess. I can feel it now.

• But it can't. Patience is only just back. You said.

• I know. I don't understand. It's never happened like this before.

• What can we do?

• Nothing we can do, hon. Just wait to see who gets picked for the torture.

• It's getting closer.

• It won't hurt, Tess. Remember, whoever is picked, it won't hurt.

• It's one of us. Joan, I don't want to go back there.

• It's all right, Tess. It'll be all …

• Joan? Joan?

• She's gone, hon.

• Alice! My name is Alice, not hon! Can you understand that?

• Hey, okay. Chill, okay?

• Where's the girl? Tess? She's not here.

• She was taken at the same time as dear Joan.

• Patience? Are you all right?

• Something is wrong. Two of us have never been taken at the same

time – and never so soon after the previous occasion.
• Why change now?
• I do not know, but I pray to the Lord that they are safe.

Lechasseur followed the stairs straight down towards the basement. Halfway down, his footsteps changed tone. He was walking on stone steps rather than on wooden ones. The sound of the cellar had changed, too. A few seconds earlier, the room had sounded cramped, his footsteps barely causing the slightest echo, but now there was a more expansive, hollow-sounding resonance from the basement. A dim, flickering oil-lamp set high on the wall ahead showed a brick archway leading from the cellar through to another room beyond. As he came level with the arch, Lechasseur could see a series of similar arches leading into the distance. Someone had gone to considerable trouble to turn all the basements on this side of whatever street this was into one huge room. He just about had time to wonder why, before the answer hit him. The pungently sweet smell was unmistakable.

Opium.

Through the archway, the scent was far stronger. The walls were adorned with threadbare, faded tapestries, supposedly Oriental in design, which Lechasseur would have bet money had never been further than ten miles from London. On one side of the arch there was a worn, old settee; a set of large, stuffed chairs filled the other side of the basement. The furniture was all pocked with burn marks, and the assorted items of smoking equipment around the basement showed the reason for the lack of care.

'Great,' Lechasseur muttered sourly. 'I'm in an opium den.' From the corner of his eye, he caught a flicker of movement in the cellar, but when he spun round to look, there was nothing to be seen.

He inspected the wick on the nearest oil lamp. It was freshly trimmed and burning strongly. The bongs were still warm to the touch. He moved carefully through the series of basements, finding the same set-up in each of the rooms.

And then he heard a slight scraping on the stone floor. Glass. Probably one of the bottles he'd seen abandoned on the floor. He hadn't been imagining things. Somebody *was* there with him.

'Hello?' he called. 'Anybody there?' There was no answer, and Lechasseur moved quickly into the next cellar. He stepped deliberately, taking swift but quiet paces. A flash of movement caught his eye. 'I can see you there,' he said, calmly and evenly. 'I'm not going to hurt you. I'm guessing you're as lost here as I am.'

Lechasseur warily stepped through the arch into the next basement. 'It's okay, nobody's going to hurt you.' He kept his voice smooth and reassuring. He panned his eyes round the cellar, and turned just in time to see a bottle flying towards his head.

- What do we do while they're not here?
- Same as we do when they're here, hon.
- I've told you. My name's Alice, not hon.
- Okay, okay.
- So you're saying we just float here until Joan and Tess get back?
- And then we float after they come back. It's not that bad.
- No?
- Well, yeah, it is. I was lying to make you feel better.
- It didn't work. The other women who are here. Do you ever talk to them?
- Some. Some don't want to know.
- This is a nightmare.
- You wish.

Emily moved warily back along the corridor. From the parlour ahead, she could hear the wireless set warming up. Through the crackles and hisses, an old tune was breaking through.

'Who's there?'

The voice stopped Emily in her tracks. It was a woman's voice, not old, but not young either. The voice was shrill and shook, as if the veneer of strength the woman wanted to project was cracking. She sounded nervous, uncertain and afraid. Whoever she was, Emily certainly couldn't blame this woman for being scared. She stepped slowly into view in the centre of the doorway, though she was careful to stay a few feet back from the door itself. There was no way of knowing how a frightened woman would react to her sudden appearance.

'Hello?' Emily repeated. 'I'm sorry if I startled you.' She stepped cautiously into the parlour, her eyes flicking from side to side, half expecting an attack from the woman in the room. Instead, she found a slim, upright woman in her fifties standing by the sideboard. Her clothes were drab and well-worn, with signs of mending here and there, but even though they were old, they were spotlessly clean. The delicate, almost reverential way the woman ran her fingertips over the assorted family photographs was more than enough to tell Emily who the woman was.

'Mrs Barton?' she asked. 'You are Mrs Barton, aren't you? This is your house.'

The woman lifted her eyes from the photograph in her hand and looked at Emily. 'That's right,' she nodded. 'I'm Joan Barton.' She turned her attention back to the photographs. She lifted one and touched the front with her hand. Her son smiled back stiffly from behind the glass.

'Your son?' Emily asked.

Mrs Barton nodded. Her gaze was centred on the photograph in her hand, but her mind seemed focused much further away. 'My little boy.' She gave a half-hearted laugh. 'Little boy,' she said wistfully. 'He was taller than me by the time he was twelve.'

'George?' Emily prodded.

The older woman looked up quickly at Emily. 'You know him? You know my George?'

'Not exactly.' Emily shuffled her feet uncomfortably. There was such an eagerness in the woman's voice when she spoke about her son that Emily didn't want to cause her any suffering by raising the subject of her son's death. But was there really a choice? If she was to find out what was happening in this house – wherever it was – Emily needed answers, even if they came at the price of causing this woman pain. 'When I got here,' Emily began slowly. 'Well, there was nobody here, but there were letters.' She nodded towards the door. 'On the table in the hall. One of them was from George's commanding officer saying how sorry he was.' She paused and took a deep breath before continuing. 'How sorry he was that George had died.' She waited for a reaction from Mrs Barton. Other than a slight slump in the shoulders, none came. The woman had obviously known that her son was dead. 'I hope you don't mind me reading it,' Emily added gently.

Joan Barton shook her head distantly. 'No. I never saw that letter. What else did he say?'

Emily sighed. 'Not much, other than that George was a good soldier, that he was brave and that he was a good man.'

'He was,' Joan nodded proudly. 'Like his dad. They both died in France,' she added bitterly, and for the first time, Emily could see how hard the woman was trying not to break down. Tears were welling and her voice was becoming choked, but a stubborn defiance wouldn't let her give in to her grief.

'I'm so sorry,' Emily said gently. 'Sit down. Please.'

In other circumstances, she was sure that Mrs Barton would have reacted to being invited to sit in her own home, but this time, Joan pulled a chair from the head of table and sat. Emily took the chair closest to her. 'Thank you,' Mrs Barton said, trying to force a smile. 'You'd think I'd be used to the idea, now, wouldn't you? It's so long since they died, but every time I come back here and see the pictures …' She looked around the room and out into the hall, as though she hadn't seen the place for a considerable time. 'The house …'

'Come back from where?' Emily interrupted.

'I don't know,' the woman shrugged, then looked quizzically at Emily. 'There's never been anybody here before, though.' She leaned forward. 'You know, when I saw you, just for a second, I thought you were my Jenny.'

'Your daughter?'

'One of them,' Joan agreed. Her eyes drifted again, becoming lost in memories. 'We had six girls before George came along. My Albert always wanted a son. Don't get me wrong,' she added defensively. 'He loved our girls. But he always wanted a son.'

Emily couldn't help but smile at the pride in Mrs Barton's voice. She had been right. This woman loved her family with every fibre of her being. 'And he got one.'

'Yes,' Mrs Barton agreed wistfully. 'And didn't he spoil the little devil something awful?'

'I think that's often the way with fathers and sons.'

'Yes,' Mrs Barton nodded. 'And sometimes mothers spoil their sons, too … just because we do.' She smiled wearily. 'Do you have any children yourself, Miss …' she stopped and cocked her head, listening. 'Did you put the kettle on?'

Emily shook her head. 'I don't think so. No, I'm sure I didn't. In fact, I took it off the hob.'

Sure enough, a few moments later, Emily could hear the whistle of a kettle coming to the boil on the stove. 'It doesn't matter.' The woman shrugged, as if a kettle boiling itself were the most natural thing in the world.

Perhaps in this world, it is the most natural thing, Emily thought.

'Would you like a cup of tea?'

The question threw Emily off balance for a second. In the middle of who knew where and with who knew what happening, she should have known that an Englishwoman would head for the tea-pot. 'You know, I think I would,' Emily replied. 'Thank you.'

Mrs Barton stood and took a step towards the door, then stopped. She looked nervously at Emily. 'This might sound strange – silly even – but would you come to the kitchen with me?'

The woman was clearly afraid of something, and Emily found it unsettling that someone could be so frightened in their own home. A home should be a haven, a place of safety, but Mrs Barton clearly felt far from safe here. Emily felt that way too. She pushed back her chair and stood, smiling as reassuringly as she could. 'Of course, Mrs Barton.'

The older woman tried to hide the her relieved sigh. 'Joan,' she said. 'Please call me Joan.'

'I'm Emily. Emily Blandish.'

Joan looked at Emily curiously. 'I haven't spoken to you before, have I?'

'No,' Emily answered, a little confused by the question. 'We've only just met.'

'No.' Joan shook her head. 'Not here.' She tilted her head towards Emily a little and whispered: 'The other place.'

'I don't follow,' Emily said. 'What other place?'

Joan straightened up. 'Perhaps you're new here,' she murmured to herself.

'Yes,' Emily confirmed. 'I only just arrived.'

'That must be it.' Joan sounded far from convinced. She looked nervously around the room and out into her hallway. 'There's never usually anyone here,' she said again.

'Not even your daughters?' Emily asked.

The reaction was as if she had slapped Joan. The older woman snapped her eyes round to Emily, but her shoulders sagged under a great weight. 'No.'

'They're not here?'

'Please don't ask me to explain,' Joan said quietly, and Emily understood that there could be only one reason for such a reaction. She remembered what she had experienced in the kitchen earlier. The bomb. The unmoving hand caught in the rubble.

'They're dead,' she whispered, half to herself.

Joan nodded, tears returning to her eyes. She pushed them away with the back of her hand. 'Three days after the telegram saying George had been killed. I'd gone out to get the rations. George was gone, but we had to carry on. What other choice was there? To curl up and give in? No, he would have wanted us to go on. I went out early to avoid the queues as best I could.' She gave a humourless laugh. 'Not that you could ever really avoid the queues.'

Joan paused, her attention slipping away into the past. 'I could never imagine being apart from my family,' she continued. It seemed as if she was talking as much to herself as to Emily. 'Even after she got married, Victoria, my eldest, spent most of her time here. Well, with Alan, her husband, away at the War, it made sense for her to stay here. We always felt safe together.'

'But you weren't?' Emily asked quietly.

Joan shook her head, and the tears she tried so hard to fight off welled in her eyes. She pulled a handkerchief from her pocket, rubbed them away angrily. 'I heard the explosion from Dock Street.'

'Your house?'

'Not exactly. The bomb landed on the neighbour's house.' Joan gestured at the wall. 'A big one. When I got back, there wasn't a house left standing in the street. It was just bricks and dust on top of a huge pit. The dust was so thick, I could hardly see. And there was smoke from the fires. The few bits of the street left standing were in flames. The fire engines could hardly get close for the rubble. Everybody was choking and coughing. The air was so hot, some of the firemen were coughing up blood.'

Joan's hands were beginning to shake as she spoke. Emily grasped the woman's hands and squeezed them. 'All of your daughters?'

'I'd gone out early,' Joan nodded. 'To beat the queues – to get some air, to not be reminded of everything about George in the house. Just to get on with life again.' She looked at Emily. 'Does that make sense?'

Emily tried to offer a reassuring or comforting smile, but couldn't force the expression onto her face. She couldn't even begin to understand what this woman had been through. If she were to be completely honest, she didn't really want to try. She had an uncomfortable feeling that it might be too much for her to bear. Perhaps, she thought, it was for the best that she had no memory of loved ones at home, wherever home might be. If she knew she was never to see them again, or that they were dead ... no, it wasn't a thought she relished.

'What happened to you after that?' Emily asked. 'How did you come to be here?' She looked around at the house.

'In a house that's obviously not been bombed or burned out?' Joan shrugged. 'I don't know. I remember the police and the fire brigade trying to stop me getting through to what was left of the house. They said it was still dangerous. But I wasn't interested in what they were saying. How could I be? I'd left my girls in the house. A couple of coppers started coming towards me, saying that I had to leave.' She laughed humourlessly. 'I threw broken bricks at them and told them to leave me alone. I was sure my girls weren't dead. They couldn't be dead. They couldn't.'

Joan took a deep breath. 'But then I saw Victoria, in the rubble. She'd been burned so badly.' Again, Joan pushed at a tear with the heel of her hand. 'I didn't see the others.'

'Perhaps that's for the best.'

'Yes, perhaps. No,' Joan shook her head firmly. 'No matter what had happened to them, I should have seen them. I should have been able to say goodbye properly before …' She waved a hand around vaguely in frustration. 'Before all this.'

Emily looked around. 'All what?' she asked.

Joan looked at Emily sadly. 'You really don't know, do you?'

Emily shook her head.

Joan sighed. 'I'm so sorry to have to tell you this, dear, but there isn't a way out.'

'No,' Emily disagreed firmly. 'There's a way in, and that means there has to be a way out.'

'We all thought that at one time.' Joan looked around at her familiar surroundings, her face an odd mixture of contempt and resignation. She still harboured a great anger, but didn't have enough will left to fight. 'But we're all trapped. All of us.' She looked Emily in the eye. 'And that includes you.'

CHAPTER FIVE

Lechasseur ducked just in time and the bottle flew by his ear, smashing against the wall a second later. He turned towards the area the bottle had come from, his hands raised, ready to fight or flee, whichever seemed appropriate. He dropped them when he saw a scrawny girl of 15 or 16 cowering back into the corner of the room, nervously eyeing the doorway, clearly wondering if she could make it there before Lechasseur.

'What did you do that for?' Lechasseur asked, keeping his voice calm and relaxed. 'Where I come from, it's considered bad manners to throw bottles at people.'

The girl didn't reply. She just eyed him, fear and suspicion equally evident in her expression.

Lechasseur took in the girl's appearance quickly. Her clothes were old and worn. The dark green skirt with the ends of petticoats showing underneath looked forty years out of date, like something from before the first War. That was a worrying thought. Had he been moved through time again? Had coming into the cellar bumped him back fifty years to Victorian London?

Sensing that this tall, dark man's thoughts were elsewhere, the cowering girl gathered her courage and made a run for the door. Lechasseur snapped back to the present – whenever it might be – and made it to the doorway three steps before the girl. She cannoned into his chest, then backed off quickly.

'Get out of my way.'

Lechasseur recognised the accent. She was London through and through. He held his hands out wide, palms open. 'I'm not going to hurt you,' he said calmly. 'But I'd like to ask you some questions, if you don't mind.'

'Of course I mind.' The girl tried to dodge round Lechasseur again, but he blocked her easily.

'I'm not going to hurt you,' Lechasseur repeated.

'I've heard that before,' the girl sneered. 'You blokes always say that, then take what you want.'

There was genuine bitterness in the girl's voice. Bitterness and anger. For all that she was little more than a child, Lechasseur was sure that this girl had seen and probably been on the receiving end of some appalling experiences. He took a half step back. 'Okay,' he said. 'If you want to go, you can. I won't stop you.'

The girl looked puzzled. 'What? Really?'

'Yes,' Lechasseur nodded. 'Really.' He stepped away from the door and leaned nonchalantly against the wall.

The girl ran.

Lechasseur watched her scoot through the archway, her heels clattering hollowly on the concrete floor. The footsteps stuttered and changed rhythm as the girl reached the stairs. They scuffed on the stone steps before disappearing completely. Lechasseur settled into one of the sofas and stretched out his legs. A few minutes later, slow footsteps came back towards the doorway. They stopped, with no-one in view. Lechasseur let a few more moments pass before speaking.

'You might as well come through,' he said. 'I know you're there.'

The girl looked through the archway at him, but said nothing.

'No way out?' Lechasseur carried on. 'I guessed there wouldn't be.'

'Never is,' the girl replied. She stayed on the far side of the arch. 'Just that blackness at the top of the stairs.'

'You've been here before? Or do you live here?'

'Live here?' the girl laughed. 'Who could afford to live here? I can barely afford to chase the dragon once a month if I'm lucky.' She shook her head. 'Nah. Chang Wu's the only one as lives here.'

'Chang Wu?' Lechasseur asked. 'Chinese? This is his place?'

'Who else would run a place like this?' the girl answered sharply. She eyed Lechasseur suspiciously. 'Don't you have Chinee where you come from?' she asked.

'Sure,' Lechasseur shrugged. 'We've got pretty much everybody you can imagine back home.'

'So where are you from?' the girl asked. 'I met some darkies before, but none of them was like you.'

Under normal circumstances, Lechasseur would have reacted to her use of the word 'darkie,' but he let it slide. There had been no malice in her voice. Only curiosity.

'None of your sort around here dress as well as you. Don't talk like you, neither,' she added. 'You ain't from round here, are you?'

'No,' Lechasseur confirmed. 'New Orleans, Louisiana.' The girl shook her head, clearly none the wiser. 'America,' Lechasseur added.

'Really?' The girl took a nervous step forward through the archway. 'I always wanted to go to America.'

'Yeah?'

The girl nodded vigorously. 'I've heard about it. The papers are full of stories about it.'

'You like reading the newspapers?'

The girl squirmed a little, slightly embarrassed. 'I can read, but not so good as some of the other girls. The ones who are really good with their reading, they tell the rest of us.' She leaned forward. 'With an 'at like that one, are you one of them cowboys?'

'No,' Lechasseur shook his head. 'Closest I've been to the Wild West is watching the latest John Wayne at the Roxy.'

'I got no idea what that means,' the girl answered testily. 'So what are you doing here?' she asked suspiciously.

Lechasseur looked around the basement ruefully. 'I'm not totally sure ...'

'Yeah,' the girl laughed wryly. 'I was forgetting you're stuck here.' She squinted slightly, as a thought occurred to her. 'Never seen a bloke here before.'

'What about Chang Wu?'

'No,' the girl said quickly. 'Not here ...' She wafted her hands around. 'Here.'

'And where is here?'

'Dunno.' She eyed him suspiciously. 'Never seen no-one before. This place is always empty when I come back, apart from some food and …' she trailed off sheepishly.

'And?' Lechasseur prompted.

'And the poppy.' The girl indicated the bongs. 'There's always some of that waiting for me.'

'Ah,' Lechasseur nodded.

'Nothing wrong with it, now and again,' the girl said defensively. She turned her body slightly, aiming a bony shoulder at Lechasseur. 'No matter what Joan says.' She glared defiantly at Lechasseur, waiting for him to argue. He just shrugged. 'It makes things easier, that's all,' the girl said. 'Makes you forget the bad things.'

'And you've seen some bad things?'

'Bad?' the girl snorted. 'You could say.' She fell quiet for a moment before continuing, 'I seen things that'd make your hair stand on end.' She stared for a moment at the smoke seeping from the mouth-piece of the nearest pipe, watching it spiral off towards the roof. 'I done some as well,' she added softly. 'That's why I come here.'

The girl was telling the truth, Lechasseur was certain of that. She had done some terrible things, and she chased the dragon to forget. Living in London for a few years, he couldn't help but have heard stories of young girls in Victorian times. These stories, added to her manner, gave Lechasseur a fair idea of what the girl had been forced to do. There were still girls in the city doing exactly the same. He ran into them with depressing regularity. 'I'm sure you had your reasons for doing whatever you did.'

The girl's shoulders slouched and she reached for the smoking pipe. 'Everybody's got to get by somehow.' She looked at Lechasseur, suddenly suspicious again. 'How do I know you won't try nothing if I have a puff?'

'Because I won't.'

'And I'm supposed to believe that, am I?'

Lechasseur's face quirked into a slight grimace. 'I hope so.'

'Here,' the girl said sharply. 'You're not funny, are you? You know.

Prefer blokes.'

'No,' Lechasseur assured her. 'But I'm old enough to be your father. Probably. So, I don't think I'll be troubling you.'

'Age don't usually stop most blokes.' The girl sounded surprised. 'In fact, the older ones are some of the dirtiest of the lot. Quick, though. They can't last long.' She stopped, embarrassed by having said so much. She studied Lechasseur's face for any sign of condemnation. His face stayed impassive. 'I'm not ashamed of what I do,' she said defiantly.

'But you're not proud of it either,' Lechasseur countered softly. 'Otherwise, you wouldn't come here to get high on opium and forget.'

'What do you know about anything?'

Lechasseur shrugged. 'What's your name?'

'Tess,' she answered, whipping the pipe from his grasp like a nervous animal taking food from an unfamiliar hand. 'Everyone calls me Tess.'

'Well, Tess,' Lechasseur tipped his hat to her. 'A pleasure to meet you. I'm Honoré Lechasseur.'

'Funny name,' Tess answered. She held the pipe a few inches from her mouth, close enough to smell the opium. To Lechasseur, she seemed uncertain about the drug, as if she wanted it there for comfort but didn't want to actually use it.

'Guess it is,' he answered. 'It's French. There's a lot of French influence in New Orleans.' He chuckled to himself. 'There's a lot of places had a lot of influence in New Orleans. It's a big melting pot of all different people and cultures. Music, food, language ... from all over the world, all mixed together in one place.'

'Sounds exciting.' Tess dropped the pipe away from her mouth. 'Would I like it?'

'Probably,' Lechasseur nodded. 'Most people do.' He sat up straighter on the sofa. 'What would you bring to the mix?' he asked. 'You're from round here, right? London?'

'Can't hide me accent,' Tess confirmed. 'Never been out of London in all my days.'

'Which aren't all that many.'

'Long enough to know there's got to be better than this.'

The strength of the bitterness in Tess's voice surprised Lechasseur.

Maybe he just hadn't expected it from someone so young and frail-looking. 'When were you born, Tess?'

Some of the wariness returned to Tess' face. 'You first.'

'Okay,' Lechasseur agreed easily. 'I was born in nineteen …' He trailed off. 'You weren't surprised when I said I was born in nineteen something.'

''Course not,' Tess answered. 'I know it's the 20th Century now. Or later, maybe. We lose track.'

'We? Who's we?'

Tess shook her head at Lechasseur's ignorance. 'You don't know a thing about this place, do you? It's …' She stopped, tilting her head to one side. 'It's coming back.'

'What is?' Honoré listened intently. Nothing.

Tess smiled. 'It's coming back. I'm going back.'

Lechasseur looked around the basement. For a moment, he was sure the girl was mistaken. Nothing was happening. Nothing was changing. Then he saw the walls. The brickwork was becoming duller, a sheen of dust forming on it. The tapestries were fading. Even the sofa he was sitting on had started to become transparent. He leaped to his feet. 'What's happening?'

Tess just smiled back at him. 'Dunno,' she beamed happily. 'But I don't mind it. It ain't that bad, really.' She spun her head towards the archway and, for the first time, Lechasseur heard the sound that had alerted Tess. Something between the wind and the howl of a dog.

'Wind?' he asked.

'No,' Tess shook her head. 'We dunno what it is, but it means we're going back.' She look uncertainly at Lechasseur. 'Well, I'm going back,' she corrected. 'Dunno 'bout you.' She shrugged. 'But you can look after yourself well enough, I should reckon.'

'Thanks for the concern,' Lechasseur said sourly. He turned towards the arch, searching for the source of the sound. It didn't seem to have any single point of origin. Instead, it was simply all around them, growing louder and more prominent. As the sound grew more intense, the trappings of the opium den faded, leaving walls and floors bare.

'Oh!' Tess was startled, and rifled in her pockets. She produced bread and cheese, and began stuffing the food into her mouth. 'I 'almost forgot,' she mumbled, spitting crumbs as she spoke. 'Got to eat while I've got the chance.'

'Don't let me stop you.' Lechasseur watched as Tess wolfed the last scraps of bread. Wherever she was being taken back to, she obviously had no fear of the place. Her eyes were dancing around the room as the whistling noise became louder. It seemed to be reaching a peak, gathering around them until it swooped closer.

A huge grin spread across Tess's face. 'I'm going home.'

Joan caught at Emily's hand. The whistling sound filled the house, coming from every room, surrounding and engulfing them.

'What is it?' Emily called, trying to be heard above the noise.

'We're going back,' Joan answered. 'It's nothing to be afraid of.'

Emily's eyebrow arched sharply. 'Then why are you so terrified?'

Joan's grip on Emily's hand tightened. 'Because every time I come here, I have some kind of hope that it'll be over. But it never is, and we always end up back there.'

'Back where?'

'Look at the house.' Joan swept her free hand in a wide arc. The sheen had gone from the kitchen, and dust was settling around them. The mirrors dulled and grime engrained itself over the house. Years of neglect appeared in seconds. A photograph on the wall slipped and tilted to an untidy angle. Even as Joan reached to straighten her husband's picture, the house was fading into darkness. 'Don't worry.' Her voice sounded hollow and distant. 'It doesn't hurt. Not really.'

As the room around them faded completely to black, the tone of Joan's voice told Emily that the older woman was clearly lying, probably more to herself than to her. She also had an oppressive feeling that she was never going to see Joan's little house again.

And then the house was gone, and there was nothing.

• Where are we?
• It's all right, Emily.
• Joan? I can't see you.
• Don't panic. You just need some time to get used to things here.
• I'm not panicking. Not yet, anyway, though it might not be far off.

• Listen to me. You're safe. You're safe enough.

• I can't feel anything. My hands. Feet. Nothing. I can't feel anything.

• You're safe enough …

• I'm sure I am. This is a fascinating sensation. Well, lack of sensation, to be more precise. There's absolutely no physical awareness at all, and yet I'm able to communicate with you. Wait, I can even … not see you as such … but I can certainly tell you're there. Remarkable.

• People don't usually adapt that quickly.

• Most people haven't had my experiences, Joan. There are others here. I can sense them. They're coming closer.

• Dear Joan, you are safe.

• Yes, I'm all right, Patience. Aren't we always?

• And you also … wait. You are not Tess.

• No. My name's Emily. Emily Blandish.

• She was in my house when I arrived there.

• This is most unusual. There has never been anyone waiting for us before.

• Joan, hon, we thought something weird had happened when you and the shrimp went at the same time.

• The shrimp?

• She means Tess.

• Yep. That's her.

• Tess? What happened to Tess?

• She was taken at the same time as you, hon.

• But she has not been returned to us.

• Tess?

'No!'

Lechasseur took an instinctive step backwards as Tess wailed. 'What? What's wrong?'

'It's going!' Tess screamed. She spun around, desperately searching the dark corners of the cellar, trying to find the sound that was fading away from around them. 'Don't go! I don't want to stay here!' She ran for an archway, her heels making a terrible clattering sound on the stone floor. Even as she reached the arch, brickwork was fading into view, and Lechasseur had to catch Tess's arm to stop the girl running smack into the brick wall that now filled the space.

'You won't do yourself any good if you go running into walls,' he said sharply.

Tess wasn't listening. She was running her fingers over the bricks that filled the archway, their faded red colouring contrasting with the dull grey of the rest of the wall.

'It can't be,' Tess muttered to herself. 'I can't stay here. I don't want to stay here.' She started clawing at the crumbling mortar between the bricks, trying to dig her way through to the next cellar.

'You're wasting your time.' Lechasseur thumped his fist against the bricks. 'Even if you could dig your way through the wall, what do you think will be there?'

'I don't know.' Tess looked fearfully around the cellar. 'But it's got to be better than the life I had here. I can't come back here.' Her voice trailed. 'I can't. I won't.'

Lechasseur reached out a hand to pat her shoulder reassuringly, but Tess flinched away. He dropped his hand quickly. He had seen fear like this among soldiers during the War. Men so on edge that they had seen everything as a threat, even their own comrades. He had even seen one pull a gun on his own commanding officer, after the captain had relayed an order taking them into battle. It had taken half a dozen men to bring him under control.

'There's nothing on the other side of this wall,' Lechasseur said, holding a matter-of-fact tone. 'No empty cellar, no opium den, no nothing.'

'There might be people there,' Tess protested. 'Well, not there so much as …' She wrung her hands in frustration as she tried to find a way of explaining the void she and the other women lived in. 'There's a place, totally black and empty, only, well, it's not empty. Not really.'

'Go on.'

'There's people there,' Tess added quickly. 'Me and Joan and a load of others. Except we're not really there.'

Lechasseur sighed. 'I don't follow.'

'Course you don't,' Tess snapped. 'You never been there, have you?' She relaxed, thinking of the void. 'We're there, even though we can't see nothing. We know we're there, though.'

'Can you see each other when you're there? You and this Joan?'

'Nah!' Tess shook her head. 'Can't even see myself. Well, you sort of can. Like it's a memory, you know? We just sort of know who's there.'

Lechasseur frowned and pursed his lips, contemplating what Tess had told him. 'A meeting of the minds?' he mused softly. 'No, nothing so mundane. Something different. Something we've no experience of.'

'What are you on about?' Tess asked. 'Did you have a puff at the poppy when I wasn't looking?'

'Just wondering out loud,' Lechasseur replied. 'I think I'm done here.' He turned sharply and headed for the door and the stairs.

'Where are you going?'

'Upstairs,' Lechasseur answered, without stopping or looking back.

'What for?'

Lechasseur stopped briefly and waved a hand around the cellar. 'There's nothing to see here. I think I've seen whatever show is going to be on here.' He pointed to the stairs. 'If I'm going to find any answers, my guess is that I'm better off looking upstairs.'

'What about me?' Tess protested. 'You're going to leave me here? On me own?'

'You can stay here if you like,' Lechasseur said. 'Or you can come with me.'

'But ...'

'But you don't know me from Adam,' Lechasseur interrupted. 'I understand that. But if you stick with me, I promise to try and make sure nothing bad happens to you. Or, you can stay here on your own. It's up to you.' He turned sharply and strode towards the stairs.

Tess looked around the cellar for a moment, a stubborn, independent streak resenting Lechasseur's manner. The sudden quiet unnerved her, but she refused to give in. Then she saw the shadows begin to move. She knew it was just her imagination playing tricks, bringing too many bad memories of too many bad experiences in cellars like this one rushing back to her. 'Wait for me.'

On the stairs, Lechasseur stopped for a moment and allowed himself a brief smirk before relaxing his face back into an impassive mask. He didn't want the girl to think he was laughing at her. 'Hurry it up,' he called. 'We don't have all day.' The black void that had sat at the top of the cellar stairs, blocking Tess's earlier escape attempt, had gone, and Lechasseur could see that the table he had moved was still in the doorway, stopping the door from closing. 'Then again,' he shrugged, 'maybe we do.'

• How many people are here?
• Around thirty, Emily. Perhaps more.
• I can tell. You're all from different periods in time.
• How do you know that?
• Joan, I have a certain … affinity with time.
• I don't understand.
• Neither do I. Not completely, anyway. But I can sense it in a way most people don't.
• I should say that's nonsense, shouldn't I?
• But you won't, Joan. You know it's true.
• I know a lot of things are true that I wouldn't have believed before.
• The people who are here with us. Tell me about them.
• You'd be better off talking to them yourself, dear.
• You know them. I don't.
• That doesn't matter. Not here. Most of them will talk to you.
• And the ones that won't?
• I …
• Joan?
• This isn't an easy place to live – or whatever you would want to call it. Everybody deals with it in their own way. Some of us talk.
• And others don't?
• Some just listen. The ones who don't talk are usually past being able to communicate. It gets to them. All this …
• Nothingness?
• Yes. We don't know for certain, but we're fairly sure some of those women who've been here longest have gone completely mad with it.

Joan Barton's favourite table was shoved unceremoniously aside, and Lechasseur strode back into the dusty hallway. He wasn't sure if he was surprised or not that it was exactly as he had left it.

'How did that happen?' Tess asked, following him out of the cellar.

'When I tried the stairs, there wasn't even a door.'

'I don't doubt you,' Lechasseur answered. 'But I think then and now are two different places.'

'Nah!' Tess was inspecting the walls and the layout of the house, getting her bearings. 'I know this house. It's the one over the top of Chang Wu's place.' She indicated along the hall. 'You come in through the back door there.' She inspected the pictures on the walls and let her finger trace the fading pattern on the wallpaper. 'It's changed a bit, though.'

Lechasseur rattled the handle to the back door, but it stayed resolutely shut. 'We're not leaving that way.' He tried the kitchen door, but that resisted stubbornly as well.

'You could try kicking it,' Tess offered helpfully.

Lechasseur offered a rueful smile. 'Tried that last time,' he commented. 'If I'm lucky, my leg should stop aching by the time I'm forty.'

'How long's that, then?' Tess asked. 'Couple of weeks?' She smirked cheekily. For the first time since he'd met her, Tess actually looked like a sixteen year old girl. Hardly more than a child.

'Smart kid,' he grumbled gruffly. 'Don't let the grey in the hair fool you. I'm not thirty yet.'

'Obviously,' Tess smirked.

'And I don't look it, either,' Lechasseur added.

'No,' Tess agreed. 'You don't.'

'Good,' Lechasseur muttered, and turned his attention to the door to the smaller parlour, where he had found the radio.

'Older, maybe,' Tess said, apparently to herself. 'Fifty if you're a day.'

Lechasseur stopped and glowered at her, but couldn't hold the expression. He smiled. 'If you're done making fun of your elders?'

'I suppose so,' Tess nodded. 'But I might start again later.'

'Great,' Lechasseur grimaced, though he noted with satisfaction that the girl's manner towards him had become noticeably more trusting. He pushed at the little parlour's door. Like the others, it stayed firmly shut. 'I'm not shoulder-charging this one, either,' Lechasseur told Tess. She had opened her mouth to answer when a creaking sound cut her off. Further along the hall, the door to the main parlour swung slowly open. Through it, Lechasseur could see only a thick, ominous darkness. He pushed an unconvincing smile onto his face.

'I've wanted to see in there ever since we arrived,' he said.

'Yeah?' Tess asked, nervously. She wasn't taken in by Lechasseur's composed act. 'Why should I be interested in what's in there?' She folded her arms and planted her feet, clearly indicating that she had no intention of moving.

'You'd rather stay here on your own?' Lechasseur asked.

'Why not?' Tess retorted. 'Better than walking into who knows what in there.' She tilted her bony chin defiantly and waited for Lechasseur to argue.

'It does feel like that old rhyme again, doesn't it,' Lechasseur said thoughtfully. He peered into the darkness, weighing up the alternatives. 'Come into my parlour, said the spider to the fly.'

'Spider?' Tess asked nervously.

'Don't tell me you're scared of spiders.'

'No,' she replied quickly – too quickly. 'I just don't like them, that's all,' she admitted. 'Horrid things, always scuttling about.' She shuffled her feet slightly, embarrassed by her confession. 'I just don't like them.'

'Me neither,' Lechasseur owned up. 'But I always guess they're more scared of me than I am of them. I hope so, anyway.' He offered a half-smile. 'I'm kinda bigger than they are.'

'I suppose,' Tess conceded.

'And I can always take a newspaper to them, but I never once saw one coming at me with a rolled up copy of the *Sporting Life*. So,' Lechasseur pointed to the open door. 'Are you coming in or staying here?'

'I don't know,' Tess said hesitantly. 'I'm not sure.'

On cue, a gas lamp at the far end of the hall flickered and died, and darkness immediately filled that space. Tess moved nervously closer to Lechasseur. They watched as, slowly, the darkness began moving along the hallway towards them, gradually engulfing the hall and its contents. Its movement was steady and fluid, like matt-black oil. It looked unstoppable. The table, a chair, walls and pictures all disappeared from sight as the darkness moved relentlessly towards Lechasseur and Tess.

'I'm guessing somebody really wants us to go into this room,' Lechasseur said softly.

Tess just nodded, unable to take her eyes from the flowing void moving towards them. Ten minutes earlier, she would have given anything to be back in the safety of the darkness. Now, she would give anything to stay clear of this black threat that was approaching. This felt anything but safe. 'All right,' she whispered. 'All right.'

'Okay.' Lechasseur grasped Tess's hand, and they stepped through the door into the dark room. Before they could react, the door swung shut behind them. 'Right,' Lechasseur mumbled. He took another step forward, pulling a reluctant Tess along with him, and suddenly they stepped from the darkness into a great, brightly-lit stone hall.

The hall was dominated by a huge wooden table covered with food and drink, above which hung an enormous wooden chandelier. A dozen or more men, dressed in Regency-style clothes, were seated around the table, and all of them were loud and drunk. Serving girls hurried around, bringing more wine and food, doing their best to avoid falling into the clutches of any of the revellers. Seated at one end of the table was a startlingly attractive young woman in her early twenties. The deep burgundy of her long, flowing dress contrasted starkly with her pale complexion, but despite her best efforts with face-powder, she had been unable to disguise completely the dark circles under her eyes. The smile on her face was obviously forced, and the way she wrung the neck of the pewter wine goblet before her showed the anxiety she was trying to hide. Her eyes flashed around the room nervously. To Honoré, it was obvious that she was hating every minute of the banquet, but that she was too afraid to say anything. *Banquet? Make that orgy*, he thought. He wondered briefly why she was so familiar to him. It didn't take him long to spot the source of her fear. As the woman's eyes scanned the hall, they always returned to the figure seated at the far end of the table. In his late forties, he didn't look particularly tall, but he was broad and powerfully built, though just beginning to run to fat. His chair was pushed back from the table, and his belly hung over the top of his trousers. He might have looked comical, but for his face. His jowly chin glistened with a mixture of sweat, spilled wine and fat from the chicken breast he was eating, but it was his small, dark eyes that told Honoré that this man was trouble. His eyes watched everything, took in every detail, working out how to use it. Most of all, he was enjoying the discomfort of the serving girls as his guests grabbed and groped at them. One girl, the same age as Tess at most, managed to avoid one pair of clutching hands but walked straight into the grasp of another drunk. Without a moment's hesitation, he pushed his hand roughly under her skirt. She screamed and struggled, finally managing to break free of her captor's grip, and lurched to the side of the hall. The man at the head of the table laughed, and threw the chicken breast at the drunk from whom the girl had just escaped.

'Useless,' he laughed. 'Too drunk even to hold onto a girl. What would your parishioners say, dear Reverend Keating?'

The Reverend belched. 'What do I care what that sort think?' His unfocused eyes ran their way blearily round the room. 'I want that girl. Where did she go?' Another serving girl, passing with a large pitcher of wine, moved too slowly to avoid the Reverend's grasp. 'Or maybe this one will do.'

'Not her,' the man at the head of the table said sharply.

'Here, Honera,' Tess tugged at Lechasseur's sleeve.

'Honoré,' he corrected. 'What is it?'

'Why ain't they seen us?' Tess asked. 'We been here a good minute or two, and they ain't said boo about us.'

'I was wondering about that, too,' Lechasseur pondered. 'It's not as if we're exactly hiding in a corner, is it?'

'Be a big corner as hid you,' Tess muttered.

Lechasseur took a step closer to the table. 'I don't think they can see us,' he said, and then, raising his voice, he spoke again. 'I don't think they can hear us.'

For a moment, Honoré thought he was wrong and had indeed been heard. The hall had suddenly fallen quiet. But the eyes of the revellers weren't on him and Tess but on the Reverend and his host. Their confrontation had become very tense, very quickly, though the Reverend was too drunk to notice. He was the only one in the room unaware of the change in atmosphere. The other men were sitting back in their chairs, either waiting for the show or trying to keep as far away from any coming violence as they could.

'I said, not her,' the host repeated. 'I think you could do me the courtesy of listening to me when you're a guest in my home.'

The Reverend slammed a hand on the table. 'I want her, Squire,' he repeated. 'And I'll have her.' He grinned, showing crooked, brown teeth. 'Or I'll damn her soul.'

The Squire leaped across the table, moving with remarkable speed for a man carrying so much girth, and swung his arm downwards, embedding a long-bladed knife into the wooden surface – straight through Reverend Keating's hand. 'I don't think you'll be able for any sport tonight, Reverend.'

It took Keating's wine-addled brain a moment to register what had happened. And then he screamed.

The Squire twisted the knife through a quarter turn. 'And when I tell you to do something in my house,' he hissed, 'you do it, or man of God or not, I'll cut your throat out and send you to Hell where you belong. Now shut up your noise, or I really might hurt you.' He yanked the knife free, and Lechasseur winced, hearing the blade scrape bone as it came out of the Reverend's hand.

With every ounce of willpower he could muster, Keating cut off his screams. He looked at the Squire in terror as his host waved the knife back and forth in front of his face. 'That's better,' the Squire said appreciatively, and wiped the blade clean on Keating's shoulder. 'Now go and get that hand bandaged, before you spoil the party.'

Keating nodded, and all but ran from the room.

The Squire turned to the serving girl who had been the unwitting cause of the trouble. 'This one's mine,' he said. 'Aren't you, Mary? A healthy little bed-warmer.' He turned his eyes sourly to the woman at the head of the table, who had remained seated impassively throughout. 'Better than my beloved wife there, anyway.' He snorted. 'But a dead sheep would be better than that lump of meat.'

His wife simply stared back, and said nothing.

'I've seen her before,' Lechasseur murmured. He moved closer to the table. 'I'm sure of it.'

Tess looked round the hall nervously, expecting to be spotted at any time. 'Where?'

'In the reception of the tower block,' Lechasseur answered. 'She was the ghost. I'm certain it was her.'

'A ghost? Let's have a look.' Tess peered past Lechasseur at the pale, fragile woman at the table. There was something familiar about her that Tess recognised. 'I think I know her an' all.'

'You recognise her?'

'Not the face,' Tess answered. She racked her brain for a way to explain what she wanted to say. 'I just know her. Who she is, I mean. It's Patience, the snooty cow I never got on with in the … well, the whatever the place is.'

'She's one of the people you're trapped with?'

'Yeah.' Tess pointed a skinny finger at the serving girl now seated uncomfortably on the Squire's lap, her face as miserable as Patience's own as the Squire's hand crept inside the front of her dress and squeezed one of her breasts in full view of the guests. 'And so's she.'

'The serving girl?'

'Her name's Mary,' Tess carried on. 'I always wondered why them two never got on. I thought it was because Patience was a toff and Mary wasn't.'

'Now you know.'

'Yeah, now I know,' Tess said sadly. 'Poor cow.' She looked from Mary to Patience and back again. 'Poor cows, both of them.'

Behind them, there was a click. Lechasseur turned, half expecting to see Reverend Keating returning. Instead, a door was open, and beyond was Joan Barton's hall. 'I think we've seen everything we're supposed to see here,' he said.

Tess nodded, and followed him towards the door. She looked back briefly at the scene in the hall, now beginning to fade. As she became transparent, Patience's head turned away from her nervous surveillance of the men in the room. Just for a moment, she seemed to lock eyes with Tess, but then she became indistinct and faded away, along with the rest of the room. Tess picked up her pace and hurried after Honoré.

CHAPTER SIX

• Your name is Sandi?

• Yeah, hon. Sandi with an 'i'. An eye for a good-looking man and an eye for a score, that's me.

• I'm not sure I know what that means. The last half, anyway.

• It means you're from a stuffed shirt era before my time, hon. I guess that's what it means.

• Perhaps. Perhaps not.

• Too bad. I was hoping to find someone else from the sixties I could talk to. When are you from?

• That's a more complicated question than you might imagine, Sandi.

• Zatso?

• Pardon?

• I mean, is that so, Emily? Your name is Emily, right?

• Yes. I came here from 1995, though I normally live in 1950.

• That's not the weirdest thing I heard recently.

• Though I have no idea where – when – I really come from.

• Nope. That's not the weirdest either, babe. Sorry. Must try harder.

• Are you always so flippant?

• Given the situation we're in, it's either be glib or go nuts. I guess you've already noticed that some of the girls here aren't paddling with both oars in the water.

• Yes. Though I wouldn't have put it in quite that manner.

- Hey-ho. You know.
- What were you doing before you found yourself here?
- Does it matter?
- It might. Do you remember, Sandi?
- Listen, hon. You really don't want to get into my past, okay?
- Don't I?
- Hell, I don't even know if I want to get into my past.
- You mean that, don't you?
- Some things are best left alone.
- Hiding from them won't make them go away, Sandi.
- But it'll stop them hurting for a while.
- What are you hiding from?
- Leave it.
- No. You had a problem before you came here.
- I said leave it!
- You may be happy to spend the rest of your life stuck in some kind of limbo, but that's far from being what I have planned for myself. If I am going to find a way out of here, for all of us, then I need to know everything, whether it's easy for you or not!
- There isn't a way out of here.
- I'm becoming rather tired of hearing people say that. Now, what were you doing before you came here? Please tell me.
- Fine. Whatever. You want to hear my sob story, I'll tell you. Okay. Me and Joe, we had a place. Not a palace, but it was good, you know?
- Joe?
- My boyfriend.
- You lived together?
- Yeah. And us not married either, huh? Go figure. We had a place, we even had jobs. Nothing heavy, just jobs to keep the cash flowing. Enough to buy food, keep the rent paid and get us a few scores.
- Scores? I don't understand.
- Scores. Drugs, okay? Pot, maybe some acid if we were feeling like it. You still don't get it?
- No.
- These drugs were more opium than aspirin, okay? Got it now? Illegal drugs that screw with the brain. Jeez, even Tess got that idea.

• Oh.

• Yeah, oh. We were doing okay, me and Joe. Then we lost our place. The landlord threw us out when Joe got busted for possession.

• Possession of what? Drugs?

• Yeah. He only had weed on him, as well. Didn't matter, though. He was guilty, and the landlord put us on the streets. It's kind of hard to find a place at short notice, so we wound up in a squat with some people Joe knew. Before you ask, a squat is an empty house where people stay without paying rent, okay?

• Yes. I understand.

• It was cold and damp, but at least it had a roof, and that was something. Joe lost his job after the bust. He spent a lot of time with a couple of the guys at the squat who were really into tripping. That's taking acid. They were major on that.

• Acid? I don't …

• It's a drug, okay? They were way into tripping on acid, and they got Joe into it.

• Tripping?

• Yeah. He got stoned a lot. I was still working, and I got pissed at him spending my money on acid. We fought a lot. Kinda ironic, huh? A couple of peace-loving hippie tree-huggers fighting all the time. I wanted us to find a place, but not him. He was happy with his new friends in the squat. He spent his time with them. I was … I was just the baggage, you know? I was just the one who brought the money. After a couple of months we weren't sharing a life.

• What did you do?

• Did I leave him, you mean? No. I loved the stupid bastard. How could I leave him? Isn't that the way with us women? We stay with them even when they hurt us? Even when we know we should leave, we still stay to try and make things better.

• Did you? Make things better, I mean.

• No. No, I didn't. Anything but.

• Go on.

• I really don't want to do this.

• I'm sorry, but I need to know.

• Suit yourself. Maybe that's the only way to be, in here – think about number one. I didn't leave him. I did the stupidest thing I could. I felt like he'd left me for his acid, so I decided to buy acid and join him. A romantic trip for two, I called it. Bad joke, huh?

• Things didn't work out the way you expected.

• That's an understatement. I bought the acid from a guy we knew. He said it was from a new supplier. Stronger stuff. Stronger than usual, he said. Sounded good to me.

• Was it stronger?

• It was different. Dirty. It hadn't been prepared properly.

• And that makes a difference?

• Oh, yeah. That makes a difference, all right. Joe was so pleased when I told him. It was pathetic, really, that I thought a trip would keep us together. But I loved the son of a bitch, and I wanted it to work, so I bought the idea. He couldn't wait to try the stuff. Just us, him and me. A Saturday afternoon. It was so sunny and warm. We could have done anything, gone anywhere. Instead, we were in a dingy old squat taking acid. He wanted to be first. I guess he was hooked and desperate for a fix. Maybe he just wanted to show me how it was done. Anyway, he dropped the acid. Straight off, I knew something was wrong. He always went really relaxed and mellow with acid. Not this time. He started having these convulsions, like he was having a fit. My cousin was epileptic. Joe looked like she did when she was having one of her fits. He was choking and gasping for breath. I shouted for help. I screamed for somebody to come.

• But no-one did.

• No. They were either out or just out of their brains. We didn't have a phone – we were a squat, we didn't have anything really – so I had to run to the phone box to get an ambulance. By the time it arrived, Joe was already unconscious and hardly breathing. He died in the ambulance on the way to the hospital.

• I'm sorry.

• Yeah. Me too. He was stupid and selfish and he could be a real piece of shit when he wanted to be, but I loved him. I really did.

• I think that's obvious.

• Is it? Then why did I kill him?

• You didn't ki …

• I bought the drugs that killed him. I killed him. I'm responsible. The police thought so, too. Reckoned I'd get ten years.

• They arrested you?

• Not on the spot. They took my name, address, details of where my parents lived … everything. They said they'd be round to see me the next morning.

• Did they arrest you then?

• Dunno. I wasn't thinking too straight, you know? I'd just killed my boyfriend. I suppose I was in shock. I was desperate, and I felt so guilty. I didn't think I could live, knowing that I had killed Joe. So I decided to do myself in as well.

• You committed suicide?

• I was going to. All the way back to the squat, I was working it out in my head. How I would do it. A scalding hot bath, dose myself up with pills and booze – if the filth had left any pills in the place – and then use Joe's razor on my wrists. It's supposed to be a peaceful way to go.

• But you didn't.

• Didn't have the chance. One minute I'm in the bath popping pills and slugging a home-brewed wine that tasted like turps, and the next – I'm here.

• Perhaps you did kill yourself and just don't remember.

• Don't you start. I was *compus mentus* enough to still know what I was doing. I didn't even take the razor apart. Wherever this is, it's not the afterlife, babe.

• I didn't think it was.

• Pity. If there is an afterlife, I'd like to see Joe again. Just to tell him what a selfish arsehole he is.

• I'm sure he didn't mean to hurt you.

• Any more than I meant to hurt him. Well, there. You've had your pound of flesh. I've told you what happened to me. Has it helped? I bloody hope so, because it's made me feel like shit.

• It's interesting.

• Thanks. I kill the only guy I ever loved, and to you it's just interesting.

• No. I mean, you came here straight after Joe died. Joan came immediately after her family were killed.

• We all have sob stories, hon. Nobody here lived the perfect life. At

least, nobody who's talked. Some of them keep quiet about their lives.
• Who?
• Snooty Miss Patience for one. She was the lady of the manor, but that's about all she'll say. To me, anyway. We don't know much about her, except that Mary was a maid in her house.
• This Mary is here as well?
• Yeah, but she doesn't talk either. She's too scared of Patience to say anything.
• That doesn't make sense. Surely everyone is on an equal footing here.
• It may not make sense to you, but to them, position is everything. Patience in particular. She wouldn't take kindly to you putting her on a level with a servant. Or with me, for that matter. And as for Tess, well, if I've pieced together the snippets Tess has let slip and put them together right, well … Patience would go ape at spending time with her.
• I don't think I'll ask.
• She had to make a living somehow. Not much of a life for someone, though, is it? Selling her body. Every night, a few quick fumbles in dark alleys just so she can afford a place to sleep. That's no life. Not even for a space-cadet like her.
• So everyone here had been living through a low point in their life when they arrived here.
• Which cliché do you want to use? Going from bad to worse? From the frying pan into the fire? They all fit.
• Very interesting. I definitely want to talk to this Patience. And Mary. I want to talk to both of them. Quickly.
• You'll be lucky. Patience avoids Mary like the plague.
• Why? I would have thought knowing someone else here would make things easier.
• Best ask them.
• I will. There must be more to it than a class distinction, though. Surely.
• Like I say, ask them. Hey, do something for me, will you?
• What?
• Don't tell anybody my little story, okay? I could do without talking about it again.

• All right.
• And don't let Joan know my suspicions about little Tess. She's got a soft spot for the kid. Treats her like one of her own.
• I won't say anything.
• You won't have to, Emily dear. I heard every word.
• Joan?
• Shit.

CHAPTER SEVEN

It hardly came as a surprise to Honoré that when he and Tess stepped through the door that appeared to lead to Joan Barton's hall, they in fact found themselves in a very different place altogether. At a guess, they were still in the same building as the hall they had just left, only now they were in a large bed-chamber, dominated by an enormous four-poster bed. The only light in the room came from a few candles in holders scattered around the walls and from the fire that roared heartily in the fireplace. A gust of wind rattled the window, and Tess almost leaped when she heard a tapping at the window.

'Branches hitting the glass,' Lechasseur explained.

'I knew that,' Tess answered defensively. All the same, she kept close to Lechasseur, keeping him as a shield between her and the window.

'Looks to be the same house,' Lechasseur mused. 'Same period, too, I'd guess.'

'For sure—' Tess agreed, before cutting off short.

Honoré followed Tess's gaze and saw Patience – the pale-skinned young woman from the banqueting hall – seated at a small table in front of a mirror, combing out her hair. She had changed clothes and now wore a long dressing-gown of a deep red silk over a gleaming white ankle-length nightdress, which was buttoned up to her neck. She looked every bit as desolate as she had in the hall. 'Patience?'

Tess bobbed her head in agreement. 'That's her. Poor cow looks

77

bloody miserable, don't she?'

'If I was married to that chap in the hall, I'd be miserable too,' Lechasseur answered.

Tess snorted. 'If you was married to him, I reckon he'd be a bit put out an' all.'

'No denying that,' Lechasseur agreed. 'Come on.' He led Tess closer to the desk where Patience had just put down her hairbrush and was staring at her pallid reflection in the mirror.

'She can't see us here either, can she?' Tess asked nervously.

Lechasseur pointed a finger at the mirror. They were standing apparently only a few feet away from Patience, but they had no reflection in the mirror. 'I guess not.'

'We got no shadows neither.' Tess was looking at the floor behind them, where her shadow should have been. She moved to the nearest candle and held her hand between the flame and the wall. The light still shone as brightly, and no shadow appeared on the wall.

'So we're not really here,' Lechasseur sighed. 'Or maybe they're not really here. I don't suppose it matters which.'

A knock at the door. Quick and agitated.

Patience looked away from the mirror, stirred from her misery. 'Come in.'

The door opened and Mary, the maid, hurried in. She moved with a shuffling, downtrodden gait and kept her eyes to the floor, unwilling to meet Patience's gaze straight on. 'Excuse me, but …'

'Get out!' Patience cut across Mary sharply, her voice brittle and shrill.

'I'm sorry, miss,' Mary whined pathetically. 'I can't. The master told me to come here.' The girl looked as miserable as Patience, and clearly wanted to be anywhere but in this room.

'I don't care what the master said,' Patience snapped. 'Does he expect me to watch while you share our bed in my place?'

'No, miss,' Mary protested. 'Please. It's much worse.'

Patience snapped to her feet and strode towards Mary. 'You're not the first little bed-warmer he's had,' she said brutally. 'He changes his kitchen whores as regularly as a civilised man changes his clothes.' She was close to Mary now, and stared hard at the girl. 'You wouldn't be the first I'd had to sit and watch him take his pleasure with,' she added viciously. 'This time next week, he won't even remember your name.'

'I think he's going to kill me,' Mary whimpered.

Patience stopped short, her tirade halted in mid-stride. 'What do you mean?' she demanded. For the first time, she was actually aware that Mary was shaking and in tears. The girl was obviously terrified. 'Why would you think that my husband would want to kill you?'

The girl didn't answer. She just shook and tried to choke off her tears.

'Any of this ring a bell with you?' Lechasseur asked Tess.

She shook her head. 'It's all new to me. But her ladyship don't exactly invite me over for tea, if you know what I mean.'

Lechasseur stroked his beard in contemplation. 'If we're here,' he mused, 'it must be important, and there must be a reason. I wonder what it is?'

• I will not talk of this with you.

• Patience, please talk to her. I know this is difficult for you, but …

• No, Joan. I will not let my life become the stuff of gossip and common discourse.

• Gossip? Have you taken a look around you? You're in limbo. Are you worried about the people here gossiping about you? Don't be absurd.

• I do not know you, Emily. But you, Joan, from you I would have expected better respect for my privacy.

• Patience, dear, I know how much you value your privacy, but I also believe that Emily might be able to help us find a way out of here.

• Nonsense. We are here and this is where we will stay.

• Or is this where you want to stay? From everything I've learned since meeting Joan and Sandi and a few others here, I'm becoming convinced that everyone here had suffered a tragedy or was in some kind of distress before they arrived here. I wonder if you're just too afraid to face your past. Or are you afraid that you'll have to go back to it if you ever were released from here?

• How dare you speak to me in that manner!

• Bluster all you like, Patience, but I want to know what happened.

• Please, Patience. I know this will be difficult, but think of the girls

here who have never had a chance of life. Don't Tess and Mary deserve their chance to have their lives back?
• I will not speak.
• Is there a chance of us getting back? Really?
• Alice?
• Yes, Joan. It's me. Is there a serious chance of us getting free?
• Emily?
• I can't promise you that it will happen, Alice, but I will try.
• That's the first thing I've heard that I've liked since I arrived here.
• Forgive me for asking, but did you have a tragedy of some kind before you were brought here?
• You could say. I assume you want the details?
• Please.
• I worked as PA for John Raymond. That name won't mean much to you, probably. But in 1995 he was one of the UK's foremost industrialists – 'captain of industry' was the phrase he loved to hear. He threatened to start wearing a sailor's cap around the office and saying things like 'Yo-ho ho'. He was a good businessman, too. And a good man. He was fun to work for, paid his workers well, treated them as equals, whether they were on the board or swept the stairs. He was also my fiancé. We'd kept it quiet, though most of the staff knew we were a couple. He was in trouble financially. There are some very jealous people in the world, Emily, and John had crossed some of them over the years. They played their part in taking him to the edge of bankruptcy, I'm sure of it. And then he died.
• He killed himself rather than be bankrupt?
• That's what the papers said, but they can go to hell.
• You don't sound so sure.
• What do you want me to do? Admit my lover killed himself? Threw himself off the top of the tower?
• Is that what happened?
• No. Yes. Oh, hell! What's the point in lying? It won't do me any good here. He left a letter, Emily. A meticulously detailed, four page letter explaining why he was killing himself and how he would be exonerated by history. It was typical John. Precise, detailed, elegantly worded. He shot back at everybody who had helped make the tower fail. It would

have shaken the country. I burned it.

• Why?

• Because if it could have been proved that he had committed suicide, I wouldn't have received a penny from the insurance company. Instead, I let his name be dragged through the mud and let his businesses – his life's work – be broken up and sold, just so that I could fill my pockets.

• The insurance company paid?

• Eventually. It had to, after the inquest recorded a verdict of accidental death. I have more money than I'll ever know what to do with, and it doesn't take away the feeling of guilt at having denied John the chance to have his last say.

• The guilt must have been terrible for you to deal with.

• Bad enough to have me thinking of doing the same as John did.

• I'm so sorry, Alice dear.

• Thanks, Joan.

• Thank you for being so honest and candid, Alice. Can I ask you one more thing?

• There's nothing more to tell.

• It's about the symbol on the building – the circle with the horns and the tail.

• Oh, that thing.

• Where did it come from?

• You make it sound important.

• It might be. Do you know anything about it?

• Of course. John designed it.

• John Raymond?

• What other John would I mean?

• He designed it himself?

• Yes. In the 1960s.

• That doesn't make sense. How could he have come up with it in the 1960s when we saw it in a much earlier time than that?

• Actually, it's not quite true to say that he designed it. He told me he saw a tramp drawing a rough version of something similar in the early 1950s. The image stuck with him and he adapted it – and adopted it – for his company logo. Why are you so interested?

• Did he ever talk to the tramp?

• No, he just watched him draw it for a while, and then ran to school because he was late. He always said he owed that tramp his fortune.

• You're sure the symbol didn't mean more to him than that?

• I knew him better than anyone. It was just a logo. Nothing more. What is it about the logo that's got you so interested?

• I saw some other people use a very similar symbol once. They weren't terribly pleasant. I have a feeling that the tramp who drew the picture was someone I knew.

• And he was involved with these unpleasant people?

• He was being hunted by them. Thank you, Alice. I was worried that they might be here, but now I think the symbol must just be the link that brought Honoré and me here. At least my mind is slightly at rest now.

• Lucky you. Are you finished with me now?

• I believe so. But I would still like to hear what happened to Patience.

• I will tell you nothing. None of you. Not even you, dear Joan.

• I'll tell you what happened.

• Mary?

• Be quiet, Mary.

• No, miss. I won't. I want out of here. I want to live properly.

• Be quiet, you insolent child.

• Patience, please be quiet. Mary, can you tell me what happened? And Patience, please don't interrupt.

The door opened behind them, and Honoré and Tess turned to see the Squire enter the room. Even in the murky light, they could see from his florid, sweating face and slightly lurching walk that he was drunk. His contorted expression showed that he was also furious. A thick leather belt held loosely in his hand trailed along the floor behind him like a tail.

'So, you're both here,' the Squire sneered. His voice was slurred and rough. 'My darling wife and my darling whore.'

'It's late,' Patience began in a reasonable tone. 'Can we not discuss this in the morning, whatever it might be?'

The belt flashed through the air, missing Patience's face by inches and catching her shoulder a glancing blow before thudding into the back of her chair. 'I think I'll discuss what I want when I see fit in my own home,' the Squire growled, watching Patience and Mary from under heavy eyelids. He circled wide around them, cutting off any chance of them backing away and penning them in.

'It's like he's rounding up sheep,' Lechasseur said quietly.

Tess nodded. 'He's enjoying it. He enjoys hurting people.' She paused for a second before continuing, more to herself than to Lechasseur: 'I've met his kind before.'

'Has she told you?' the Squire asked his wife. 'Has she told you her little secret?' He spat the last word as if it were a curse. 'The filthy slut's secret.'

'I haven't said anything,' Mary whined. 'I haven't.'

Despite the dull throb from her shoulder, where the belt had struck, Patience kept her voice still and calm. 'What secret would that be? I'm sure it is nothing that need cause concern.'

The Squire snorted and spat on the floor. 'She's done the one thing you haven't managed to do. For all your breeding, you've not done the one thing you were brought for. No,' he corrected himself. 'The one thing you were *bought* for.' He waited a moment, hoping to see Patience flinch. She disappointed him, remaining stoic under his gaze. 'How does it feel,' he pressed on. 'How does it feel, to know you're less use to me than a common serving wench?'

• What did he mean by less use than you, Mary?

• I don't know anything about the lives of the master and his wife, but he had wanted a son for a good number of years. His first wife died bringing a daughter. They say she was a weak infant and didn't last long.

• So he married again to have a son?

• Yes, Miss Emily.

• Just Emily. And Patience didn't provide this heir.

• No, miss.

• I think I see where you've been leading with this. Patience couldn't get pregnant, but you did.

• Yes.

'The maid is bearing your child?' Patience's back stiffened and her calm manner became obviously strained. 'This common nothing?'

'A common nothing who's managed to do the most basic woman's job,' the Squire snapped back. 'Something you never showed an appetite for.'

For the first time, anger bubbled through Patience's calm veneer. 'I thought I was brought here to be your wife, not a breeding animal to provide you with children.'

'What else would I need a wife for?' the Squire replied sharply. 'But you're not even fit for that.' He flexed his arm, and the belt danced dangerously. 'I wonder if you're fit for anything. You've been a waste of money as a wife.'

'I am not a possession,' Patience hissed.

'You're bought and paid for!' the Squire roared. 'Your father had a title but empty coffers. I paid him well for you. A dowry, he called it. I say it makes you as much a possession as the cattle in my fields. Do you say different?' He pushed his face close to Patience. She fought down the nausea she felt every time his familiar stench of stale sweat, ale and tobacco came near her. 'Do you?'

'No,' she answered quietly. In truth, she had given up any hope of her marriage being a good one even before the ceremony had taken place. The match had been arranged by her father, and it had not been her place to object.

'I never thought as she'd take being treated like that,' Tess muttered.

'What else can she do?' Lechasseur replied. 'She's terrified. They both are.'

'At least now you will have your precious heir,' Patience said bitterly. She barely had time to register that the belt was flying towards her before she felt the leather lash her back.

• He went mad.
• The villain sounds mad already.
• Please, Joan. Let her finish. Go on, Mary.
• He said my baby wouldn't be an heir. How could a maid's bastard be his heir? He had a position to keep. He couldn't say that he was the father of my baby. Said he wouldn't take the chance as I would tell

people, either.

• He wanted you to get rid of the baby?

• He wanted to get rid of me. He was drunk. I don't think that mattered, though. He was an evil man, whether in his cups or sober. He wanted to kill me. He wanted to kill me for carrying his baby, and he wanted to kill the mistress for not carrying it. He was going to kill us both. All three of us.

'Stop him,' Tess pleaded. 'Do something.' The belt sliced through the air and struck Patience's back again.

'What can I do?' Lechasseur's hand was balled into a fist in impotent rage. 'We can't touch these people. We can't change what's happening.'

'There must be something you can do,' Tess protested. She rounded on him. 'What bloody good are you if you can't stop this?'

'We're not really here, remember?' Lechasseur retorted. 'Besides, I think this is what really happened to Patience and Mary. For some reason, someone wants us to see it.'

'I don't want to watch it,' Tess protested. 'Not again.'

'Again? You said you didn't know what had happened here.'

'Not them,' Tess mumbled. 'It's too much like how my dad killed my mum. I don't want to see it again.'

'You saw that?'

Tess nodded. 'And I ran, 'cause I know he'd have gone for me next. He was always quick with his hands – and his belt.' She looked back to the scene in the bedroom as the belt arced down onto Patience's shoulder.

Patience winced but didn't make a sound. She glared defiantly at her husband. Her refusal to scream, to acknowledge the pain he was causing, was a small victory. He recognised the defiance and brought the belt crashing down again.

Mary had backed herself against the wall, torn between protecting herself and defending Patience. 'Stop. Please, stop.'

Tess was visibly shaking. 'Please make it stop.'

Lechasseur would have liked nothing better than to have snatched the belt from the Squire's hands, but he knew there was nothing he could do. In frustration, he lashed out a hand at the Squire, but watched in anger as it passed through his target's shoulder. 'Why do we have to watch this? If there's a reason, let us know!' he yelled at the ceiling.

'There's no need to shout.'

Tess yelped in surprised fear and hid behind Honoré's body, but Lechasseur spun at the familiar voice. 'Emily!'

Behind them, Emily was fading into view in the room, accompanied by a matronly woman of around fifty whom Honoré didn't recognise. 'You almost sound pleased to see me.' Emily smiled, but she looked tired. 'You weren't worried, were you?'

Lechasseur feigned nonchalance. 'I knew you could look after yourself.'

Emily's smile became warmer, and the affection was clear in her voice. 'I was worried about you, too.' She looked past Honoré to the scene being played out in the bedroom. The Squire, now breathing hard, brought his belt whipping down across Patience's back again. Her dressing gown and nightdress were now both torn open, and her bloodied back was clearly visible, showing the scars of the previous beatings she had endured.

'You're next,' the Squire snarled at Mary. He raised the belt high over his head, ready to deliver another brutal blow. He stopped in mid-swing, drunk confusion on his sweat-covered features, as, slowly, Patience and Mary faded out of existence in front of his eyes. He looked around, perplexed, searching for proof of some kind of trickery, but as far as he could see, he was now entirely alone in the room. He fumbled through making the sign of the cross, his hand clumsy at the unfamiliar action. 'Witches,' he muttered. 'Witches.' He ran to the door and yanked it open. 'Witches,' he screamed, loud enough to wake the house. 'The witches have gone!'

He ran through the door, his voice and footsteps diminishing as he ran. As the sound of his passage faded, so did the room around Honoré, Tess, Joan and Emily, and they found themselves abruptly back in the great hall of the manor.

Emily glanced at Tess curiously. 'Who's your friend?'

'This is Tess.' Honoré answered. 'Tess, say hello to Emily.'

Tess bobbed her head in a nervous greeting and did as she was told.

'Hello,' she said.

'Tess?' Joan stepped out from behind Emily and stared at Tess, a mixture of curiosity, warmth and surprise on her face. 'You're Tess?'

Tess nodded. 'Joan?' In her mind, Tess had created an image of Joan, the warm and maternal figure her own mother had tried but never quite managed to be. In person, Joan didn't disappoint her friend.

'I've often wondered what you looked like,' the older woman breathed. 'You're hardly more than a child.'

'I'm ...'

'Hush.' Joan grabbed Tess into a huge embrace, and held her for all she was worth. After a moment's shock, Tess relaxed and let herself return the hug. The first genuinely affectionate contact she had experienced in longer than she wanted to remember. Perhaps the first she had known in her entire life. 'Never mind, dear. These people think they can get us free from here.'

'I don't know if I want to leave,' Tess said uncomfortably.

Joan stiffened. 'What do you mean? Why would you want to stay?'

Tess squirmed under Joan's gaze. 'I never been hungry here, and I don't have to spend every minute looking over my shoulder, worrying as I'm going to be attacked.' She shrank away from Joan slightly. 'And I don't have to do nothing ... Well, I don't have to do nothing I'm ashamed of, just to get by.'

'Sandi said some things,' Joan said slowly. 'Terrible things about what you did. I don't want to repeat them.'

'Don't matter,' Tess sniffed. 'They're probably true.'

'Oh.'

The disapproval and disappointment on Joan's face didn't come as any surprise to Tess. She had seen those expressions a hundred times before, whenever people found out what she did to survive. Even pick-pockets, muggers and murderers had looked down their noses at her. She had learned quickly to shrug and to grow a thick skin. 'I understand if you don't like it. Really.' She tried to sound as if the woman's censure hadn't affected her at all.

Joan Barton most assuredly did disapprove of Tess's profession, but she was intelligent enough to know that there were reasons why girls fell into that business. Any anger she felt was aimed more at the society

– and the villains – who would push a girl into selling herself. In the end, this was just another child who needed to be looked after. 'It doesn't matter, does it?' she said. 'It doesn't change who you are.'

'But it does tell you why I don't want to go back.'

'Yes,' Joan answered, and she hugged Tess again, amazed at how skinny the child was. 'But we'll be all right. We will.'

Honoré looked away from the exchange between Tess and Joan. He had no inclination to intrude on a private moment. 'Who's *your* friend?' he asked Emily.

'Joan Barton.'

The name rang a bell in Lechasseur's head. It took him only a moment to place her. 'Her name was on the letters. Her house?'

'Yes,' Emily nodded. 'It wasn't just her son who was killed in the War, Honoré. It was her entire family. Her son, her husband, her daughters … all of them.'

'Jesus,' Lechasseur breathed. 'And she's still worrying about the kid?'

Emily glanced briefly at Joan and Tess. 'I think she's taken Tess as a sort of ersatz daughter.'

'I suppose that makes sense,' Lechasseur agreed. 'They obviously care about each other. God knows, the kid needs somebody to keep an eye on her.'

'They've all had terrible experiences, Honoré,' Emily said with feeling. 'All of them.'

'That's the reason they're here?' Lechasseur mused.

'It would be an enormous coincidence if it wasn't,' Emily agreed.

Honoré rubbed his chin thoughtfully. 'I don't think this is natural, though. I think something brought them here.'

'Are you turning religious on me?' Emily asked.

Honoré grunted a small laugh. 'My mother wishes,' he answered wryly. 'No, it's the way we've been moved around here, like somebody's been trying to explain something to us without actually saying anything. Show not tell, you know?'

'I know what you mean,' Emily agreed. 'I've been thinking along similar lines myself. But if that's the case, why are we here now?'

Lechasseur's mouth quirked into a grimace. 'I'm not sure about that,' he responded. 'I've noticed something, though.

'Tess,' he called. 'Tess.'

Joan looked up as Lechasseur spoke. 'Your friend is calling for you,' she told Tess.

'I heard.'

Joan peered at Lechasseur with just a hint of suspicion. 'Emily never said that her friend was a coloured.'

'I was worried about that, an' all,' Tess replied. 'But he's all right. I heard stories about darkies in Africa eating people, but he's a nice enough sort. Never tried nothing on with me. Not even when he found out ... well, when he found out what I used to do.'

'I haven't really met many coloureds,' Joan said uncertainly. 'But I'm sure he's all right,' she conceded.

'He's better than all right, Joan,' Emily answered sharply. 'He's my dearest friend, and he's far from deaf.'

'Oh.' Emily was pleased to see that Joan at least had the decency to blush at being caught in her racism. 'I'm sorry, Mister ...'

'Lechasseur. Honoré Lechasseur.'

'Interesting name,' Joan answered, forcing a smile.

'It's French,' Tess said. 'But he's from America.'

'Really?'

'Yes, really,' Emily answered irritably. 'Look, if you're quite done, can we deal with what brought us all here? What was it you wanted to ask Tess, Honoré?'

'This room,' Lechasseur cast a hand expansively around the room. 'Do you see anything different about it since the last time we were here?'

Tess shrugged. 'The table's cleared – apart from the dust. The fire's out. Oh, and there ain't so many candles.' She looked at Lechasseur expectantly, feeling quite pleased with her observations. 'Is that it?'

'Higher,' Lechasseur pointed to the walls. A series of portraits now hung at head height at regular intervals around the walls. Each of them contained the image of a different woman.

'They weren't here before,' Tess said, and stepped towards the closest picture, her shoes clacking on the stone floor.

'That's what I thought.' Lechasseur sounded reassured.

'Honoré.' Emily was standing on tip-toes, peering closely at one of the framed pictures. 'These don't look like paintings at all. Come and take a look.'

It took only a moment for Lechasseur to see what Emily had spotted. 'I see what you mean,' he said softly. 'They're more like photographs than paintings.'

'Exceptionally high quality photographs,' Emily commented. 'Look at the clarity of the features on these women.' She pointed out a woman dressed in coarse woollen clothes. Her hair was matted and dirty, her face unwashed. Rotting black stumps and sickly brown teeth showed in her open mouth. 'And how could there be a photograph of someone from the middle ages?'

Tess had made her way along the line of pictures, inspecting the women in the frames with interest. She stopped as something caught her attention. 'This one's empty,' she called.

'There's another empty one here,' Joan answered from the far side of the hall.

'Why leave two of them empty?' Lechasseur asked. 'It doesn't make sense.' He followed Emily to the next picture.

'Unless there's something we're overlooking,' she answered, taking in the elegant but pale face of a woman in a Regency-style dress who peered down, eyes filled with sadness, from the picture above. 'Patience.'

'Definitely,' Lechasseur agreed.

Emily moved to the next picture. Another familiar face looked sadly back at her. 'And Mary.' She hurried on along the line of pictures. 'I think these are all images of the trapped women.'

Lechasseur picked up his speed to keep pace with her. 'So the two empty frames would be for …' He pointed to Tess and Joan.

'Yes,' Emily agreed. 'I think so.' She peered at the next picture, that of a woman in full ancient Roman regalia, her hair intricately curled up on top of her head. Only a slight crook in the nose where it had been broken and a haunted look in the eyes stopped her from being jaw-droppingly beautiful. Next to that picture hung another frame, but this one was different again from the rest. It hung down to floor level and there was no picture inside, yet it wasn't blank either. Instead, there was a dull grey sheen that reflected only a small fraction of the light that hit it, casting a dull glow that reached just a few inches from its surface.

'What do you make of this?' Emily asked.

'Not much of a mirror,' Lechasseur answered absently. 'It even makes me look good.'

'As if you don't think you're the most striking man in London,' Emily scolded.

'Striking?' Honoré sounded offended. 'I was thinking handsome at least. Possibly even dashing.' He ran his finger along the edge of the frame, but was unable to get any kind of purchase behind the wood. He waved his hand in front of the dimly reflective surface. A murky blob waved back.

Emily sniffed. 'Dashing? Not exactly the word I would have …' Lechasseur's yell cut Emily's reply abruptly short. 'Honoré? What is it?'

'More of a who it is,' Lechasseur said, stepping away from the mirror. 'I'm looking in a mirror, but that sure isn't me.'

A small boy was in the mirror. No more than five or six years old, he had an untidy mop of hair, so dark it was almost black, and bright, clear blue eyes. He wore a grey shirt and black britches that looked like they had seen better days – and several previous owners. His black shoes were similarly worn, and showed signs of having been mended by someone who was less than expert at the task. There was something Victorian about him, and Lechasseur was reminded of the movie about Oliver Twist that Emily had recently dragged him along to.

'I've seen him before,' Emily said. 'He was the boy I glimpsed on the stairs in Joan's house.'

'I believe you.' Lechasseur replied. 'I think I caught sight of him in the cellar at an opium den.'

'He gets around, doesn't he?' Emily eyed the boy suspiciously. 'And I won't ask what you were doing in an opium den, Honoré.'

Lechasseur peered at the figure closely. He knew what Emily was thinking. Was this the same boy – the boy that was not really a boy – that they had encountered before, in 1950? He couldn't be sure.

Inside the mirror, the boy's eyes swivelled and locked onto the small group staring at him – and then he began to walk towards them. He grew larger inside the picture, and the background faded into the far distance until he was life-sized. He raised a hand and held it flat, as if touching his palm to the other side of the mirror. Then he calmly stepped through into the room.

CHAPTER EIGHT

• Miss Patience. Miss Patience.

• Go away, Mary. I have nothing to say to you.

• I had to tell them, miss. I had to …

• You had to do as you were told and know your place.

• I know my place isn't here, miss. This isn't a place for anybody. I want to get out of here.

• Back to my husband's bed?

• No.

• Do you think your bastard will make you lady of the manor?

• No. I know what the Squire will do if he finds me. But I'll take my chances. I know the house. I can find my way out.

• Then what?

• I got family. They'll look after me and the baby.

• They will disown you and throw you into the street.

• Not everybody has the same morals as you gentlefolk.

• Mind yourself, girl.

• Why? We've been here forever, and you treat me like your husband treats the dogs. Worse, even.

• I treat as is your place. A slut who used her body to try to take my position from me.

• You think I wanted that pig anywhere near me? Do you think I enjoyed what he did? I didn't have no choice. Not any more than you did.

• Do not compare your predicament to mine.

• Why not. I didn't want to be in his bed, but I didn't want to be on the streets either. I didn't want my family thrown out of their cottage because your husband was their landlord. I didn't want to be pregnant, and I didn't want to be pregnant for however long we've been here and knowing every minute that I'd never see my baby. I didn't want the beatings he gave me when it took his fancy, either. I didn't want any of it. Did you think of that? Did you?

• I have nothing more to say, Mary.

• Fine.

The room fell absolutely quiet as the boy stepped through the frame of the picture and coolly looked at the four people gathered around it, scrutinising them, almost if he were weighing their reactions to him. He looked at each one in turn, but held his gaze on Tess just a little longer than the others and offered her the hint of a slightly shy grin. This didn't go unnoticed, particularly by Tess, who moved until she was partway blocked from the boy's view behind Joan, and then nudged at the older woman until they were both watching from behind Lechasseur's shoulder.

'Are you afraid of me?' the boy asked. His voice was quiet but clear and had just a hint of London to it. 'You mustn't be afraid of me,' he went on. 'I shan't hurt any of you, I promise.'

The statement worried Emily. If the boy – assuming he really was a boy, and given their recent experiences she was not at all convinced – was promising not to hurt them, the clear inference was that he *could* do so if he chose. 'Who are you?' she asked.

The lad sniffed, and scrunched up his face a little. 'That's a difficult question.'

'Why?' Emily continued.

'That's a difficult question too.'

Emily sighed. 'Do you know who we are?' she persevered, determined to get an answer of some kind from the boy.

'Oh, yes. I know all of you.' The boy was pleased to have an answer finally, and gave it eagerly, speaking quickly, his voice rising with excitement. 'Some of you better than others.'

Lechasseur tilted his hat back on his head as he appraised the boy. 'I'm going to assume you're not just a little kid, right? What are you?' he asked bluntly. 'Are you the same creature we met before?'

Lechasseur's brusque tone made Joan Barton bristle. She had spent her entire adult life caring for children, and this stranger's manner with the boy clashed with her instincts to protect the child. 'Don't frighten the lad,' she said, before leaning towards the boy so that her head was almost on a level with his. 'Are you a special little boy?' she asked kindly.

A quizzical look danced across the boy's features. 'That's what you called your son, isn't it? You called him your special little boy.'

Joan pulled back, as if the boy had slapped her. 'Yes. Yes, I did.'

'Was he special?' the boy continued, clearly oblivious to the discomfort he had caused the woman.

'He was special to me,' Joan answered.

'Is that why you were so unhappy when he died?' Again the question was asked blandly.

'Yes.'

'Were you sadder when he died than when your other children died?'

Joan's voice was barely more than a whisper. 'No.'

The boy persisted. 'Was one child worth more than the others? Did he mean more than the others? Was he more important?'

'No.'

'Would you have swapped them for him?' He sounded genuinely intrigued by the idea. 'How many of their lives would you have given for his?'

'Stop it,' Joan demanded.

But the boy was clearly fascinated by his subject. 'Or would you have let him die to save them? Is six better than one?'

'Stop asking me these things.'

'Stop it!' Emily had seen enough. She moved until she stood between the boy and Joan. 'Stop it right now.'

'Don't be angry.' The boy's voice was almost a whine. 'I need to ask questions so that I can know things.'

'If we answer your questions, will you answer ours?' Emily asked.

'I might,' the boy answered cagily. 'But me first. I want to ask first.'

'All right,' Emily agreed warily. 'What do you want to know?'

The boy's brow puckered into a frown. 'I'm not sure,' he answered. 'I was really just wondering if you would let me go first.'

'Will you tell me something?' she said, trying to avoid the tone she would take if she was talking to a child.

'Where do you come from?' the boy asked suddenly.

'Where do I come from?' Emily parroted.

'Yes,' the boy nodded. 'Where do you come from?'

'Well,' Emily said thoughtfully. 'London.'

'No,' the boy answered impatiently. 'No, you don't. Where do you *really* come from?'

'Do you mean what year?' Emily prodded cagily.

The lad stamped his foot. 'No, I do not mean what year. I didn't ask what year, did I?' he snapped petulantly. 'I asked you where you came from. *Where* is a place. *When* is a time, and I didn't ask when, I asked where.' His chin jutted forward and his bottom lip stuck out defiantly. 'So, where are you from?' he repeated.

Emily was surprised to find that she wasn't certain what to say. In the time since she had arrived in London, Emily had developed any number of flippant lines to explain her mysterious past. Somehow, none of them seemed appropriate here. Nor did simple denial. This boy – or whatever he was – knew more about Emily than he had let on, she was sure of that. Did he, she wondered, know anything about who she really was – or at least who she had once been? Emily squared her shoulders. 'I'm not certain of where I come from,' she said honestly. 'I have no memory of my life before I arrived in London in 1949.' She waited for a reaction.

The boy simply nodded. 'It must be terrible not to know who you are,' he said.

'I didn't say that,' Emily responded. 'I know who I am now, I just don't know who I was before.' Even though she knew she shouldn't ask the question, Emily couldn't stop herself from adding, 'Do you know anything about my past?'

'Depends what you call past,' the boy shrugged. 'If you go back to

1950, this will be your past, but then the past will be the future.' He giggled. 'And that's silly.'

Honoré laughed, humourlessly. 'I've been saying that since we started this time travel business.'

The boy tilted his head to look up at Lechasseur, and for the first time, Emily could see that the boy had a dusting of freckles across his face. 'I know what happened to you when you were a soldier,' the boy said, as plainly as if he was discussing what Lechasseur had eaten for breakfast. 'I know about the explosion.'

Lechasseur bristled. The movement was subtle, but Emily knew him well enough by now to recognise when he was becoming defensive. 'Do you?' Lechasseur replied, his voice not as even as he would have wished.

'Oh, yes.' The boy's head nodded. 'I know lots about you. About the things you did when you were young – when you were a boy. The things you did when you were growing up, meeting girls ...'

Emily interrupted. 'You seem to know an awful lot about us.' Too much for her liking. 'Why don't you tell us who you are?'

'My name, you mean?' the boy blinked.

'Yes.'

'I don't have a name,' he answered.

'Don't be daft,' Tess moved from behind Joan. She had seen plenty of things in her life – and in the past short while – to terrify her, but she found that she wasn't afraid of this little boy, no matter how he had come to be here. She had seen boys like him on the streets all of her days – all bluster and bravado but, at heart, desperate to be hugged by their mum. 'Everybody's got a name,' she said in a friendly voice.

'I don't,' the boy answered. 'I don't need one.'

'Then what will we call you?' Emily asked.

'Why do you have to call me anything?'

Emily's mouth flexed in a puzzled little grimace. 'Because it's easier to have a name we can call you. It's what we're used to.'

'What do you want to call me?'

Emily shook her head. 'It's not for us to decide.'

'Isn't it?'

'No,' Tess interrupted. 'It's for your mum to do that.'

'But you're not an ordinary little boy, are you?' asked Emily.

The boy beamed, as little boys do when praised for being clever or funny or special.

'No,' continued Emily, thoughtfully. 'So why do you look like one?'

The boy scowled disappointedly at Emily. 'You're very pretty, but you're not nearly as clever as I thought you were. You've had all the answers put in front of you, and you haven't worked it out yet. I should send you back and let someone else come.'

'No,' Emily all but yelped, then she calmed herself. 'I mean, no. I want to work this out.'

'All right,' the boy agreed. 'But if you don't get it right soon,' he added petulantly, 'I'll send you back to where you came from.'

'Right now, 1950's looking pretty welcoming to me,' Lechasseur muttered.

The boy looked disappointed with Lechasseur. 'No,' he said sourly. 'That's not where I saw you.'

Emily looked sharply at Honoré. 'It *is* the same creature we saw with Barnaby. It must be!'

'The creature the Cabal had trapped,' Lechasseur said. 'But we freed it,' he protested.

Emily turned her gaze back to the child in front of them. 'I'm right, aren't I?' she asked. 'It was you that was trapped by the cult, wasn't it?'

The boy leaped up and down on the spot and clapped his hands with excitement. 'I knew you'd work it out,' he exclaimed. 'I knew you'd work it out, and I knew you'd be able to help me.'

Lechasseur was taken off guard slightly. 'How can we help you?' he asked.

'Why do you need our help?' Emily picked up the questioning. 'We know how powerful you are. We saw that the last time we met.'

Lechasseur nodded. 'Tracking down people who were time sensitive so that they could be killed.'

The boy shifted uneasily. 'They made me do that. I didn't want to. Really.' He sounded almost pleading.

'Of course you didn't,' Joan said kindly, and Emily wondered if the older woman really understood that what seemed to be a cheeky young boy was really something very different. Whether she did or not,

Emily marvelled at the woman's ability to put aside the pain the boy had caused and offer him kindness in return.

'But you did have the ability to bring all these other people here,' Emily stated.

'Assuming they're real,' Lechasseur offered. 'And not some kind of scam he's pulling.'

'I hadn't considered that,' Emily admitted.

'Hey,' Tess protested. 'What d'you mean, "if we're real"? Course we're bloody real, aren't we, Joan?'

'Of course we're real,' Joan said quickly. 'And don't swear, Tess. I've told you before.'

'Sorry,' Tess apologised automatically. 'But he was saying we wasn't real,' she continued. 'And we are real. As real as him.'

'I know.' Joan squeezed Tess's arm reassuringly. 'He was just thinking out loud, weren't you, Mr Lechasseur?'

'I guess so,' Honoré admitted.

'You see?'

'Well,' Tess said sourly. 'Think quieter next time.'

Emily tried to pull the conversation back on track. 'If we've confirmed that everyone is real,' she said to the boy, 'maybe you'd tell us why they're here.'

The boy smirked. 'Can't you work it out?'

'Because they were unhappy? Because something bad had happened to them?'

'That's it,' the boy nodded. 'They were all sad or unhappy. They'd all had something really bad happen to them, or something really bad was going to happen to them. Some of them were going to be killed or to kill themselves.'

'So you brought them here?'

The boy nodded.

'To protect them?' Emily asked.

Again a nod.

'But why only women? Why no men?'

'It was men who made me hunt those people. Men hurt me, and men were hurting those women. Men always hurt people. They always have.' Small blue eyes turned to Lechasseur. 'Even him. He killed people in his war. I could stop men hurting those women and …' The voice cut off abruptly, a slightly guilty look appearing on the boy's face.

'And?' Emily pressed. 'And what?'

'And I thought one of them might be able to help me.'

'But they couldn't?'

Another nod.

'So you brought us here, too?'

'That's right.'

'But if you're powerful enough to bring all of us here, and create all of this,' Emily waved a hand around the room, 'why do you need us to help you?'

'And what exactly do you want us to help you do?' Lechasseur asked suspiciously.

'I can't move,' the boy said. 'I should be able to move through time. I should be able to be anywhere in time or space, but I can't.' The boy was becoming agitated and upset, with frustration and anger creeping into his voice. 'There are worlds you can't imagine out there. Worlds of water, worlds that are all gas, some that are ice. Some of the worlds have people on them. People who talk in songs and by thought and by colour. Some of them are kind, and others only want to kill. I've seen them wipe out planets, blow planets up even, but I've also seen art and beauty and amazing animals.' The boy looked desperately at Emily. 'I was trapped in 1921,' he pleaded. 'And when I escaped, I was only able to reach as far forward as 1995. Now I'm trapped here. I can reach out to other times in the past, but can't go to them.' Again his voice caught with frustration. 'I can almost feel them, but they're just out of reach.'

'You want us to help set you free?' Lechasseur asked.

'Please,' the boy pleaded. 'I can't stand being trapped. Please let me be free again. I want to move between suns again. I want to see new worlds. I want to feel the universe dissolve around me as I move through the time fields. I want to be free again.' Tears were welling in his eyes. 'You can't imagine how it feels. To have been able to go anywhere, to be at any point in time, and to have it all taken away from you. To be trapped in one place. You can't imagine.'

'I spent over a year in bed after the War,' Lechasseur said quietly. 'For a while, I couldn't see anything except walls, and then they moved my bed so that I could see out of the windows, and that was worse. I could see the sunlight and smell the flowers and the grass when it was freshly cut. But I couldn't touch it. I couldn't pluck a flower to sniff it or walk in the grass or feel the sun on my face.' He shrugged self-consciously. 'It's not the same exactly, but maybe I understand a little.'

'Then you'll help me?' the boy asked uncertainly.

'If we can,' Lechasseur glanced at Emily. 'Right?'

'If we can,' Emily confirmed.

The boy started speaking quickly, as though afraid they would change their minds if he didn't hurry. 'I know how to do it,' he blurted. 'It's those things you call time snakes. They're the answer. They reach through time, backwards and forwards. They cross barriers in time. They're the answer.'

'They're how we travel,' Emily said swiftly, trying to slow the boy's onslaught.

'I know,' the boy went on. 'And they have huge amounts of energy in them, because of the way they weave through time. If I can have that energy, I can break loose and be free again.'

'You want to tap someone's time snake?' Emily asked. 'How is that possible?'

'I can do it,' the boy said with certainty. 'I know how to take someone's time snake.'

'Snake?' Tess asked nervously. 'I don't like snakes. I seen a couple on the common. I hate them.'

Lechasseur raised a hand to quiet Tess. 'These aren't snakes like you think of them,' he explained. 'It's just a phrase to describe something that might look similar.'

Tess still looked far from convinced. 'If you say so,' she muttered. 'But I wish you'd called them something else, that's all.'

An uneasy chill spread through Emily. 'You said you could *take* someone's time snake,' she said. 'If you take someone's time-snake, what will happen to them?' She knew she wasn't going to like the boy's answer.

'They'll unexist,' the boy said, in a flat, matter-of-fact tone.

'You want to murder someone?' Joan choked.

'No,' the boy said. 'You don't understand. They just won't exist

100

anymore.' He turned to Emily. 'Make her understand.'

Emily shook her head. 'I can't,' she said. 'I don't think I understand it myself.'

'Setting aside the hows and whys,' Lechasseur interrupted slowly, 'I think we're missing one important question here.' He let the room quieten for a moment before finishing. 'The who. Just who is he expecting to … to unexist?'

The question hung uncomfortably in the air as four pairs of eyes turned to look at the little boy. 'It's none of you,' he squirmed.

'Who then?' Joan asked.

'One of the women you brought here?' Emily asked. 'You said you wanted to help them. Is this how you want them to pay for your kindness? By giving up one of their lives?'

'That's stupid,' the boy snapped. 'I could have made any of them unexist if I wanted to. I could have just taken their time snakes any time I liked. I could have, and nobody would have known.'

'So why didn't you?' Lechasseur asked.

'Because I don't want them to unexist.' The boy was becoming agitated again. 'I don't want that. I want them to carry on.'

Lechasseur shifted uncomfortably. 'If it's not any of them, that leaves only two options.' He pointed at Emily and then at himself.

'No, it's not you either. I don't want anybody who's alive.'

'Well, you can't kill 'em when they're dead,' Tess sniped, then caught herself. 'Can he?' she asked.

'No,' Emily assured the girl. 'Even he can't kill people who are already dead.'

'I dunno why, but that's a relief,' Tess muttered.

'Oh, god.' Emily's haunted whisper quietened the room completely. She looked at the boy with horror. 'It's not the dead you want, is it? It's exactly the opposite.'

A smile began to pull at the boy's mouth as the pieces of the puzzle finally came together in Emily's mind.

'You want the unborn,' Emily breathed. 'You want the baby. You want Mary's baby.'

• Sandi?

• Yeah?

• What will you do if you get back to your own time?

• Dunno, Alice. What about you? What will you do in '95?

• I'm not sure. But I know I won't commit suicide. It's odd, but I've realised from being here that I want to live. Really live. I'll grieve for John, but I want to have a life.

• I'm not sure what I'll do. I don't know what I can do. But if I'd gone to jail for … for what I did, I'd have been out fifteen years ago. Maybe I've served my time.

• More than that, by a long way.

• If things do turn out, maybe I can look you up in '95.

• Why not?

• I'll be a middle-aged hippie, probably driving a van.

• Painted garish colours?

• Natch.

• Do you think we will get home?

• Well, you know how to kill any cheery atmosphere, don't you?

• I'm serious. Can we escape?

• Escape? No way, hon. But this Emily character has ideas, and things are kinda weird around here right now.

• I'd have thought things were weird here all the time.

• No. Things normally have a pattern here. They're kinda dull most of the time, but things are changing. Two people disappearing at once. This Emily showing up and then disappearing again. Hell, even Mary stood up for herself. No, something's happening. Patience has been here longer than me. Ask her.

• Patience? Patience?

• Patience?

• I am sorry. My thoughts were elsewhere. What did you say?

• Sandi was saying she thought something was happening.

• And Alice wanted to know what we'd do if we all got home.

• Home? If I ever return home, I think I will surely be murdered.

• You're kidding, right?

• I think I would prefer death to a return to the life I had.

• What about Mary?

• I have been unfair to the girl, Alice. I have thought only of myself and ignored her suffering. Perhaps I will be able to help her, though I doubt if she will allow me to do so. And in truth I have no idea how I could help her.

'You want to kill a baby?' Joan said. Her voice was shrill with horror. 'That's disgusting.'

The boy backed away a few steps. 'I wouldn't be killing it,' he whined.

'But you would be taking its life away,' Emily countered.

'It would unexist.'

'And what about Mary?' Emily pressed. 'Shouldn't she be here? Surely she should have a say in this?'

'Mary?' The boy looked confused. A thin finger pointed at Tess. 'Not Mary. It's her baby I want.'

CHAPTER NINE

- Mary?
- Leave me be.
- Jesus, I've been here forever, and that's the first time I've heard you say boo to a goose.
- Leave me alone, Sandi.
- Well, that's a step forward, hon.
- What are you talking of? You never say anything that makes sense. Instead you sneer and make jokes and hide behind insults, and I am in no mood for you.
- Well, little miss quiet's found a backbone.
- Don't insult me! You chose to make your life a hell. Your choices did that. I had no choice in my life. No choice to how my life would be. No choice to whose bed I was dragged into. No choice but to be seen as his whore. No choice when I fell pregnant, and no choice when he took his belt to me when he found out. Your life was of your making, mine was forced upon me as surely as he forced himself on me when I took his eye. I wasn't a servant. I was a slave. Better I was a slave in the Indies. At least then I'd be long gone from him.
- I'm sorry. I didn't know.
- Why should I be loud about my shame? So that you could all whisper in the darkness, calling me the same names you call Tess when you think she will not hear? No. It's none of your concern.

- So whose concern is it? Yours?
- Mine
- On your own?
- Yes.
- Bad news for you. Being a martyr is out of fashion.
- Don't make fun of me.
- I'm not. Really. I'm not. But you don't have to deal with everything on your own.
- Leave me alone.
- Listen.
- Go away! Please leave me alone!

'Don't be bloody stupid,' Tess exclaimed. 'I'm not pregnant. Mary's the one as is knocked up.'

The boy's head shook. 'No, she isn't. She lost her baby when the Squire beat her with his belt.'

'Of course you're not,' Joan agreed. 'You're far too young.'

'Yeah,' Tess said softly. 'Too young for a lot of things, but I done them anyway.'

Lechasseur stepped towards Tess, but Emily caught him and shook her head. Whatever the girl had to say could prove to be vital, no matter how painful it might be.

'I didn't set out to be on the streets,' Tess continued. 'That wasn't what I wanted. I had dreams when I was little. Such dreams. Dreams of being in the countryside. They always used to talk about it. My mum said it was always sunny in the countryside, and everything always smelled sweet.'

'Did you ever go?' Emily asked. 'To the countryside?'

'Nah,' Tess answered sadly. 'Never had the money to go.' She snorted derisively at her memories. 'Never had the money to go anywhere more than a half dozen streets away, really, except that bloody waste of time to see the Queen. Never expected to go anywhere either. I didn't mind. Well, I was a kid, I didn't know nothing else. It was okay when Mum was there. Dad could be a drunken sod sometimes – more than sometimes. He worked down the docks. Made good money, then. But he had a taste for the drink. Drank his wages, so sometimes we didn't eat, and when Mum got to him about it … well, he was as quick to hit her as he was to belt me.' Tess's voice caught bitterly. 'Then one day she narked him too much about it, and he went for her. He beat her, and he kept beating her till she stopped moving. Till she stopped breathing.' She sniffed. 'Then he just went. Never saw him again.'

'He left you?' Emily asked. 'Alone?'

'Yeah. Probably for the best, really. I don't think I could have watched him hang. Not even for that.' Her voice trailed off. 'Even though I hated him for all the things he done to Mum. And to me.'

'How could he do that?' Joan asked, obviously both distressed and disgusted by the story she was hearing. 'How could he murder his wife? How could he abandon his child?'

'How old were you?' Emily interrupted. She shared Joan's revulsion for a child being left in that situation, but didn't have time now for Joan to make an emotional scene.

'Eleven,' Tess answered. She sounded relieved that Joan had been interrupted. 'And I was out on my ear as soon as the landlord found out my folks was gone. An eleven year old's not going to be able to pay the rent.' She gave a humourless laugh – a laugh too cynical for someone of her age. 'Well, that's what I thought. But I either had to look after myself or wind up in the poor-house, and I wasn't going in one of them places. I'd learned a few things. I knew how to make things disappear without anybody seeing.'

'Stealing? You were a thief, too?'

Tess bristled at the condemnation in Joan's voice. 'I didn't take much,' she said defensively. 'And nothing from nobody who couldn't afford it. Just a few things here and there – a few things off a stall, a few flowers from a basket. I didn't need much to afford a room for the night. I did all right for a while.'

'You got caught?' Lechasseur enquired.

'Yeah,' Tess nodded. 'Not by the police. I'd just lifted a bag of chestnuts. He was on the other side of his cart. I didn't think he'd see. He bloody saw me all right. He grabbed me and shook me half out of my skin. Then he went for me with his belt, worse than anything my dad ever done to me. The police saw what he was doing, but they didn't do nothing. Didn't want to get hurt themselves, probably. I knew then

I couldn't stay on the streets. Then this woman offered me a place to stay, regular food and some coin in my pocket. So I took it. I knew who she was and I knew what kind of place she had, but I must have been so stupid. I never thought they'd want me to … to do that.'

'You were a kid,' said Lechasseur.

'That's not an excuse for being stupid,' Tess snapped angrily, though her anger was clearly aimed entirely at herself rather than at Lechasseur. 'I didn't know some blokes liked them young. I didn't know much, did I?' she spat bitterly. 'I screamed all through the first time. He just kept telling me to scream more.'

'You don't have to tell anybody this.' Lechasseur looked square at Emily, challenging her silently to disagree. She said nothing, but Tess continued. Other than a few slips, she had kept the truth hidden to herself for over a century, and now that she had started telling the story, she didn't seem able to stop.

'Took weeks for me to stop screaming and crying when they sent somebody to me. I wanted to run away, but I had no place to run to. So I let them do what they wanted.'

'How long?' Joan floundered, searching for something to say.

'Till I started growing up,' Tess answered angrily. 'They didn't have no use for me once I got hair on it. Their men didn't care for that, so they threw me out and dragged in some other poor cow.'

'And you were back on the street?' Emily pressed.

'No home, no family, and I couldn't do nothing to earn money, so I did what they'd made me do. Wasn't all that bad.' Tess tried to sound nonchalant about the experience, but succeeded only in letting her anger show. 'A couple of times a night and I'd have enough for a place to stay and something to eat.'

'Except you hated it?' Lechasseur asked. 'That's why you started taking opium.'

'You think anybody could be happy with that life?' Tess spat. 'The poppy just made it go away for a while. I'd used it off and on since I started, you know.' She paused briefly as another wave of unpleasant memories came to her. 'And it made the pain stop after, well, after I'd seen the … midwife.'

'Midwife?' Joan demanded. 'You said you weren't pregnant.'

'I'm not. Not any more. I was – happens to us all, I suppose – so I saw the midwife to get rid of it. God, it hurt.' Her voice cracked as she remembered the filthy back room, illuminated only by two candles, and the black-toothed midwife holding the long, pointed spikes she had used to get rid of the baby. 'I'd have been better seeing a butcher.'

'How could you kill your baby?' Joan Barton's voice was calm and quiet. Tess had expected Joan to scream or shout or strike out at her. She would have taken any of those things ahead of the cold condemnation she heard in her friend's voice.

'It wasn't a baby,' Tess protested. 'Not yet. It wasn't born or nothing. I couldn't have a kiddie. I didn't have enough to look after myself. I didn't even have a room. How could I look after a kiddie?'

'You just find a way.' Joan's voice rose with anger. 'You just do.'

'How?' Tess shot back. 'With what? I couldn't go on working if I was showing, could I?'

'You could have done something,' Joan snapped. 'You didn't have to kill your baby. Don't you know how precious a child is?'

Emily moved between Joan and Tess. The story was told now, and she had as much information as she could get from it. There was nothing to be gained from letting the situation deteriorate further. 'She knows, Joan. Look at her. She's still a child herself.'

Angry tears welled in Joan's eyes. 'I lost seven children, and she casually throws one away like a rag.'

'I didn't just throw it away,' Tess screamed back. 'I just didn't want it havin' the same life as me.'

Joan's face twisted with rage, resentment, disappointment and bitterness. 'Stay away from me. Just stay away from me.' She turned her back to the room, angrily wiping her eyes.

The room fell quiet for a long moment, letting the storm pass until Emily spoke.

'Honoré,' she sounded puzzled. 'If Tess did away with her baby, why does our little friend here think she's pregnant?'

The boy had watched silently as the scene had played out before him, quiet bemusement on his face. 'Because she is,' he said, as if it was the most obvious thing in the world. 'The midwife didn't get rid of both babies. Only one.'

'What?' Tess croaked.

The boy offered his gap-toothed smile again. 'You were expecting twins.'

Tess's voice was hollow. 'I'm still expecting?'

'Yes,' the boy nodded cheerfully. 'You're expecting me.'

'How can I be expecting you? You're not a baby.'

'I was,' the boy answered. 'Or I will be. Or maybe I won't.'

'You're lying,' Tess hissed. 'I got rid of it. You're lying.'

The boy shook his head defiantly. 'It's the truth. I am what your son will be.'

'I don't have a son!' Tess yelled. 'I don't want no baby.'

The boy began to cry. Tears streamed down his cheeks, and his shoulders jumped in time to his sobs.

Joan rounded sharply on Tess, her anger spilling over again. 'Tess, how can you be so cruel to ...'

'To a child, Joan?' Emily interrupted. 'Remember, he's not a child,' she said evenly. 'Just something that's taken the appearance of what Tess's son would look like.'

Tess sniffed back a tear, and looked to Emily and then to Lechasseur. 'Is it true? Am I still expecting?'

Lechasseur glanced quickly at Emily. She nodded briefly, and he turned back to Tess. 'I don't think he'd lie – he needs you to be pregnant. The only way out for him is to kill ... to unexist ... your baby.'

'But I can't be pregnant.' Tess' voice was tired and she sounded lost. 'I can't.'

Emily placed a comforting hand on the girl's arm. 'You are – and I think that's what your son would look like.'

'God almighty.' Tess stared at the boy with a mixture of horror and wonder. 'I've been pregnant all this time. With him?'

'Yes,' Emily confirmed.

'That's my baby?' Tess continued, as though unable to quite grasp the idea.

'Well, that's what he'd look like,' Lechasseur said.

Tess said nothing, but couldn't take her eyes from the small, black-haired boy looking up at her. A dozen emotions pulled at the girl. She looked as if she might hug the boy or strangle him or run screaming as far as she could. Emily wouldn't have been surprised if Tess had done all those things and more. Instead, she simply stared at the boy.

'Does raise a question,' Lechasseur said to Emily, 'how Mary will react when she realises she's not pregnant. Poor kid.'

'So, will you do it?' the boy demanded impatiently.

'What?' Tess had stopped paying attention to the room and was still staring at the boy.

'He wants to know if you'll give up your baby,' Emily said quietly.

'Tess, you can't …' Joan began, but the boy interrupted her quickly.

'Of course she can,' he sniped. 'She's already done it once.' He turned to Tess. 'And look at her. She's right. She can't look after a baby.'

'She'd find a way,' Joan responded.

'No, she wouldn't,' the boy said quickly. 'She's too much like her father for that.' His voice became softer, more persuasive. 'Her father was a drunk who couldn't handle having children. She's sixteen, and she's already half way to being a drunk. She'll be completely addicted to opium by her next birthday. Do you really think that's someone who's fit to be a mother?' The boy had been speaking to Joan, but everyone in the room knew that the question was aimed squarely at Tess.

'I think she has a right to find out,' Joan said firmly. 'She has the right to know what it's like to …'

The boy cut across Joan. 'Be quiet,' he said sourly. 'In fact, we don't need you here at all.'

Joan got as far as saying 'I …' before she faded from sight.

Emily turned sharply to the boy. 'What have you done with her?'

'Is she safe?' Lechasseur demanded.

The boy smirked at them cheekily. 'If you're so clever, what do you think?'

CHAPTER TEN

• Joan? That is you, isn't it?

• Yes, it's me.

• I'm glad you're back. Sorry if that sounds selfish.

• I think I'm becoming used to people being selfish.

• What do you mean?

• It doesn't matter. What's happened here?

• Mary the mouse just gave Patience an earful.

• About what?

• She wants out of here. She wants to take her chances on getting out and escaping, whatever we have to do. Says it's for her baby.

• That poor girl.

• Yeah. Must be tough having a kid but knowing she won't see it.

• No. It's not like that. She doesn't know … Dear God, how can I tell her that her baby's dead? I can't do that to her. I can't take that away from her.

• How did the baby die?

• Patience?

• Forgive me if I startled you, Joan. How did Mary's baby die?

• When your husband beat her, apparently.

• He was a foul man with an evil temper. He took a whip to me for not falling pregnant, but beat Mary because she did. In truth, he never really needed an excuse to beat people. He hurt them because he enjoyed doing so. He would relish the misery he has caused – and the pain Mary will feel when she hears of her child. I should take the duty of telling her this news.

• But you can't.

• I think she would take the news easier from another, if such news can ever be easy to take.

• I'll do it.

• Thank you, Joan. I am grateful for the kindness.

• It's not much of a kindness, is it? But if we're going to be leaving here, she has to know. She can't go on thinking she's pregnant.

• We're leaving?

• You're not pulling our chains, Joanie? We are getting out?

• It depends on Tess, but I think she will agree to what has been asked of her.

• That's great.

• Is it, Sandi? I think she'll regret it for the rest of her life.

'You'll do it, won't you?' the boy looked expectantly at Tess. 'It won't hurt, I promise.'

Tess kept staring at the boy. 'I never wanted a kiddie,' she said softly, more to herself than to anyone else. 'I couldn't hardly look after myself, let alone a little baby.'

The boy nodded keenly. 'That's why you went to that midwife. This will be much easier. You only have to say yes, and it'll all be over and everyone can go home.' There was a pleading in the boy's voice, giving it a thin and reedy tone. 'Please.'

'He's a beautiful little thing, inne?'

Lechasseur gripped Tess' bony shoulder firmly. 'This is not your son.'

'Honoré's right,' Emily agreed. 'Always remember that this is not really your baby.'

'I know that. It's just how my baby would look. No,' she corrected herself. 'It's how he's gonna look. It's weird. I never really thought of it as a person before. Not a real one. Well, it wasn't, was it? Just a thing. An idea in my head, but not a real person. That's how come I could let it go so easy. But I can't let him go. Not now as I've seen him.'

'You have to help me,' the boy protested.

'She said no,' Emily replied firmly.

'But she has to,' the boy shouted.

'No!' Emily raised her own voice in reply.

'I'll kill them,' the child threatened. 'I'll kill them – and you too. If she doesn't help me, I'll kill them, one by one, until she does agree.'

'Why would you do that?' Emily asked.

'Because she won't do what I want, stupid,' the boy snarled.

'You brought these women here, and you've kept them safe for all this time,' Emily mused quietly.

'Time doesn't matter to me,' the boy answered.

'We both know better than that,' Emily countered quickly. 'And these women matter to you as well. You've cared for them, protected them. Why? Because you were made to suffer?'

'I wanted to help them.' The boy sounded pleading. 'Why won't they help me? It's only fair.'

'Fair doesn't come into it when you're talking about lives,' Lechasseur interjected. 'Sometimes life isn't fair and you just have to accept it.'

'But she already tried to get rid of her baby once,' the boy whined.

'A long time ago,' Lechasseur said.

Emily said firmly, 'You're not taking her baby's time snake.'

'That's not for you to be saying, is it?' Tess spoke up. 'He's right. I did try to do away with him. My baby. It's why I started going to the poppy-house. First it stopped the pain of what she done to me, and then it stopped me remembering what I done.' She reached out a hand to touch the boy's hair but stopped, as though afraid she might damage something precious. 'But it's my decision, isn't it? I have to decide if this thing can have my baby. It can't. My life's been a mess. Sometimes, I made mistakes; other times, I paid for other people's mistakes. But I never had a chance to fix a mistake before. I do now. Look at him. That's what my boy's going to look like. Maybe I can't give him the best life in the world, but I can give him the chance to have a life.'

'You can't do that,' the boy squealed. 'You have to give it up. You have to.'

Despite the trouble he knew it was going to cause, Lechasseur felt a wave of relief at Tess's decision. The idea of handing over a baby's life as a barter make his skin crawl. 'It's her choice.'

The boy's face reddened with anger, and he looked as if he might stamp his feet with child-like fury. 'I'll kill them all.'

'Will you?' Emily asked mildly. 'I don't think so. You don't want to kill anyone.'

'I don't want to stay trapped, either,' the boy shot back. 'They'll come for me. They'll find me and trap me worse than this. I won't be trapped any more. You were supposed to help.'

'We can't help you commit murder,' Emily stated flatly.

'Maybe I'll just take the baby's time snake,' the boy challenged. 'Maybe I'll eat all their time snakes.'

Emily stood unmoved. She wouldn't back down or give in to childish threats. 'If that's what it takes,' she answered calmly. 'But you don't want to do it, do you? You don't want to, or can't, take the life of someone who won't willingly give it.'

'I've been responsible for too many people dying,' the boy answered quietly.

'That's it, isn't it? You're trying to make amends for the deaths of all those others, the deaths you caused under instruction from the Cabal.'

'I didn't want to have anything to do with that. You have to believe me.'

'I do.' Emily gave a sad, humourless smile. 'But it still doesn't make this right.'

'I won't stay trapped.' Desperation had returned to the child's voice.

'And we won't let you kill an innocent baby,' Emily responded firmly.

'What will you do to stop me?'

'We'll find a way.' Emily hoped she sounded more confident than she actually felt.

'Don't make me hurt you.' There was a desperation among the threats.

'You can't have Tess's baby,' Lechasseur said.

'I'll take it if I have to.'

'No, you won't,' Emily said calmly. 'You'd have done that by now if you were going to. That's why you brought us here, isn't it? So that we could persuade Tess to give up the baby and you could go free with a clear conscience.'

'I need to be free!' the boy screamed at her. 'You have to agree!'

'We won't give up a baby's life,' Emily reiterated. She looked at the boy and thought for a moment. 'What about the life of someone who threw their life away?'

Emily's question took the boy off guard. 'What?'

'Someone who committed suicide,' Emily answered.

'Who?'

Honoré looked at Emily curiously, wondering what she was going to say.

'The man who built the tower.'

The boy looked thoughtful.

'Well?' Emily pressed. 'Will you take his life in exchange for the infant's?'

'Emily.' Lechasseur grabbed Emily's arm. 'You can't do this,' he hissed. 'You can't just give away someone else's life.'

'I didn't.' Emily pulled her arm free. 'He gave his life away when he committed suicide.'

'But he had a life before that,' Lechasseur argued angrily.

'And Tess's baby has a life in front of him,' Emily snapped back. 'And he deserves his chance to that life.'

They stood, staring at each other, neither willing to back down. 'Taking one life to save another isn't justified, Emily,' Lechasseur said grimly.

'I know,' Emily agreed, and the expression on her face left Lechasseur in no doubt that she understood – and was agonised by – the implications of what she was suggesting. 'I don't really see an alternative, do you?'

Lechasseur felt his shoulders slump. He suddenly felt tired and old and truly impotent. 'No,' he agreed sadly. 'But that doesn't mean I like it.'

'Neither do I,' Emily whispered. She took a deep, brisk breath, then turned to the small boy. 'If you take the man who committed suicide by leaping from the top of this building in 1995 ...' She waited for a reaction from the child. When none came, she carried on quickly, '...

you can have his time-snake, and you'll be set free.' The boy's eyes gleamed brightly. 'And you have to release all these women,' Emily continued. 'You understand that?'

The boy nodded eagerly. 'I will,' he promised. 'I'll let everybody go. Them, you …' He bit his lip sheepishly. 'I was only trying to help them,' he said earnestly. 'I only wanted to make sure they weren't hurt.'

'I understand,' Emily nodded. 'But if you're going to do this, you had better do it now.' Her voice sounded brittle and bitter, despite her best efforts at keeping it firm. The idea of condemning someone to die – to have never lived – didn't come easily to her.

'All right,' the boy agreed. 'I'll do it now.'

'Wait a minute,' Tess objected. 'Are you leaving?' she asked the boy. He nodded. 'I have to.'

'I will see you again?' Tess asked uncertainly. 'Well, not you exactly …'

'Your baby will be fine,' Emily said sharply. 'Now just let him go.'

'All right.' Tess reached a hand towards the boy, as if afraid she might break him – or that his touch might burn her. With a force of will, she touched her hand to his head, and was rewarded with a cheeky smirk. Encouraged, she ruffled his untidy hair. She was trying to put some kind of order into the unruly, jet-black mop when the lad faded away from under her hand. Tess turned to Emily and Lechasseur for an explanation, but kept quiet as she saw the angry looks passing between them.

'I hope you know what you're doing,' Lechasseur said coldly.

'I know what I'm doing,' Emily replied, and just for a brief second, her face showed Lechasseur that she had a plan. 'I know what I'm doing,' she repeated. 'I just don't know if it'll work or not.'

CHAPTER ELEVEN

Year: 1995

With a single, deliberate pace, John Raymond stepped off the roof of his tower block and began to plunge to his certain death. He had regrets that it had come to this, but there really was no other way. Oddly, he felt slightly disappointed that he wasn't terrified by the sight of the ground hurtling towards him or by the knowledge that he was about to die. He didn't know quite what he had expected, but he had anticipated more than this feeling of the wind grabbing at him. It was quite calming, really. He closed his eyes and prepared for his end.

Had anyone been standing at the foot of the building, they would first have seen the dreadful sight of a man plunging towards a sickening death on the pavement, but then something even more remarkable. As the man passed the windows of the second floor, which contained the offices of a graphic design company, his body faded out of existence. He simply vanished into nothingness, leaving no hint that he had ever thrown himself from the roof.

Year: 1980

Bartelli's Restaurant was as busy as its exclusive clientele ever allowed it to be. There were few tables in the restaurant, and those were well spaced apart. Gianni Bartelli knew that his customers usually relished their privacy, and he made sure they got it. He also made them pay through the nose for it, but both he and his customers knew the arrangement, and it suited them all very well.

Bartelli moved through the restaurant, circulating as he did every half hour or so. He started no conversations but nodded to his customers and let them get on with their meals.

This evening, the restaurant was almost full. In the centre of the room, a knighted actor was at a large table with a big party of friends. Nearer the window – at a table they had chosen,, Bartelli assumed, in case a press photographer should happen to look in – were a young footballer and his page 3-girl fiancée. Seated towards the back, in a corner near the kitchens, Bartelli spotted John Raymond having a quiet dinner with an attractive, red-haired woman in her mid thirties. The rose on the table by her hand and the intimate glances indicated that this was not a business meeting, so Bartelli gave the table a wide berth. He returned to his office and resolved to work out the stock orders for the next week. Moments after his door closed behind him, John Raymond, his lady guest and the table they had been seated at all faded out of existence. Half an hour later, when Gianni Bartelli did his next flesh-pressing circuit of the restaurant, he had no memory of a table being in the corner that night, and he certainly had no memory of a man named John Raymond.

Year: 1965

A tinny radio was playing the latest Beatles single, and that suited Ringo Doyle right down to the ground. The success of his market stall was based almost completely on the fab four. He sold suits like they wore, shirts like they wore, and even copies of their records – cheaper than the shops, too, though admittedly these copies may have accidentally fallen off the back of a lorry before finding their way into his possession. To complete the Beatles feel, Doyle had abandoned his own name of William in favour of Ringo, certain that his nose and cheeky manner gave him a resemblance to Ringo Starr. He even affected a Scouse accent, though he was actually from Manchester. Business was decent for Doyle, but he knew it would be positively booming if he had a slightly better pitch, and he even knew which pitch he wanted – the one that pushy weasel John Raymond had. He threw Raymond a filthy look, but Raymond paid him no heed. He never paid Doyle any heed – he was too busy giving his patter to the punters. One day, Doyle assured himself. He'd get the pitch one day.

As a customer stopped to inspect a grey suit on his stall, Doyle slipped into chirpy Scouser mode and started his banter. With his attention distracted, he didn't see John Raymond and his stall slowly fade out of view. In fact, nobody saw it happen. When Doyle turned back, peeved at not having sold the suit, he spotted the empty space in the market.

'Now why the hell isn't somebody in that space?' he wondered, and began shifting has stall.

Year: 1950

At first glance, the man looked no different from any one of a hundred men who sat on the pavement, sketching and trying to sell their drawings for a few pennies. The War had ended, but people were still struggling to get by any way they could. John Raymond had seen plenty of other artists like this one, trying to sell hastily-sketched portraits. He usually passed one on his way to school every morning. This one was different, though. He didn't seem interested in selling his work, and when John moved closer, he saw that the man was sketching the same thing over and over again. A circle with little marks at the top. It looked sinister, and John held back nervously, which was unusual for such a confident boy, but he couldn't just walk away either. Unsettling as the image was, he felt drawn to it as well. The horns at the top made him think of a dragon, and John sidled a few feet closer to get a better look.

Hearing the scuffing of feet, the artist turned to look for the source of the sound, but he turned a fraction of a second too late to see John

Raymond wink out of existence.

In the hall of portraits, there was an uncomfortable, expectant silence. Emily, Honoré and Tess all knew that something would happen soon, but none of them knew precisely what it would be or when it would happen. Tess had tried asking a few questions, but had given up after being first ignored and then given a terse glare by Emily. Confused and more than a little lost, she wandered around the room, examining the portraits. She stopped at the image of Joan and felt an ache that she had hurt her friend. Guilt wasn't something Tess was used to feeling – she had learned early in life that it was an emotion she could ill afford – but she desperately hoped she could find a way to make things right with Joan. She would sort things out with Joan. She didn't know how, but she would do it somehow.

For a moment, she thought that the smearing and blurring of the image's edges were an illusion caused by the tears in her eyes, but then she looked at the next portrait. Patience's sad yet beautiful face was beginning to melt and slide as well. She turned to Lechasseur and Emily.

'Over here,' Emily instructed, and Tess scampered to her obediently as slowly the room around them melted and dissolved.

• Naw, hon, you got it wrong. Tess isn't knocked up. That's Mary.
• No, she's not. She's not pregnant at all.
• The slut has lied to us all this time?
• It's not like that, Sandi.
• All the time she's been here she's been carrying a dead infant in her, believing him to be alive. And it was my my husband who caused this.
• Jeez, Patience. I guess someone ought to tell the poor girl.
• Joan here has kindly offered to do so.
• That's real nice of her, hon. But I'm not sure it's gonna work out.
• Mary deserves to hear the truth of her situation.
• Maybe, hon. But maybe not now. In case you guys haven't noticed, things are changing hereabouts. I'm starting to see colours.
• She's right, Patience.

- Yes, I see. Red and blue.
- And gold.
- Orange. It's like a rainbow breaking through.
- And I can see you. Dear Joan, I can see – surely that is you?
- Yes, it's me. Can you take my hand?
- I don't know. You don't appear to be real.
- Try.
- We're all becoming solid, hon.
- There. I'm not … wait. I can feel your hand, dear Joan.
- Sandi, you take my hand, too.
- I had never thought I should feel the warmth of another human being again.
- Hon, it must be true – we must be getting out of here.
- At what cost for Tess, I wonder?
- Worry about Tess later, hon. Look around.
- Dear Lord.
- Christ almighty, there are dozens of us, Joan.
- There are yet more becoming visible.
- I had no idea there were this many of us.

'We've got company.' Lechasseur was looking past Emily.

She turned and saw the entity wearing the appearance of Tess's son. He faded into view as the room around them continued to dissolve and melt, and he had an enormous smile on his face, as though he had just been given the best Christmas present ever.

'It's working.' The boy was almost bouncing. 'Can't you feel it?'

'You're breaking free?' Lechasseur asked.

'I can feel this place letting me go.' The boy spun about the room, oblivious to the walls melting and fading around him.

Emily cut across the creature's revelry, her voice brisk and business-like. 'In that case, it's time for you to keep your end of the bargain,' she said. 'Release all the women you're holding.'

The boy looked disappointed, as though Emily had said something extraordinarily stupid. 'Obviously,' he answered. 'I'm doing it already.'

Emily heard the women a few seconds before she saw them.

'Ghosts,' Tess muttered. Emily put a comforting arm around the girl, and wondered at how such a bony, under-fed child could possibly be pregnant.

'Not ghosts,' Emily said reassuringly. 'Friends. Most of them,' she added.

A small, filthy girl in her late teens, dressed in coarse animal skins, was first to appear. Her eyes darted around the room in terror. She snarled, baring yellowing teeth, and backed her way around the room, but then stopped, looking past Lechasseur in amazement. He turned to see a middle-aged woman fading into view behind him. Then another woman appeared by her side. Then another and another ... Through their materialising bodies, he could see the walls of the room still becoming increasingly insubstantial.

'We might need a bigger hall,' he muttered to Emily. 'It's getting crowded in here.'

'I know. It's time to send them all back to their own times,' she told the boy. There was no answer. His eyes were out of focus and his mind was somewhere – or somewhen – else. 'Listen to me.' Emily grasped the boy's shoulders and shook him. 'Listen,' she repeated. 'You have to send them home before you can go. You agreed to that. Are you listening?' She shook the boy again. 'Are you?'

'Hey,' Tess pulled at Emily's shoulder. 'Leave him alone.'

'Be quiet,' Emily snapped, never taking her eyes from the child. 'You must send these women back. You must.'

The boy's eyes slowly turned to her, and he began to focus. 'All right,' he said softly. 'I did promise, didn't I?'

Emily nodded. 'Yes.' She indicated the petrified women filling the room. Some stood alone, while others huddled together in the hope of finding safety in numbers. 'They're all afraid here. They don't know what's happening to them.'

'But if I send them back, they'll be afraid there, too.'

'Probably,' Emily agreed. 'But it's better for them to live whatever lives they have in their own times than for them to be trapped forever. You understand what it's like to be trapped, don't you?' The boy nodded. 'You wouldn't want anyone else to feel that, would you?'

A huge sigh escaped from the boy, and his shoulder slumped. 'No,' he said sadly. 'I'll send them back now.' He closed his eyes and began to concentrate, his mind seeking the familiar paths that flowed through time.

Standing beside Lechasseur, Tess had spotted Joan Barton as soon as she had appeared back in the room. Even though her instinct was to run to her friend, she stayed in Lechasseur's shadow.

Honoré leaned close to Tess's ear. 'If you want to say something to her, say it.'

'Nah.' Tess scuffed her feet uncomfortably. 'She said some rotten things about me.'

'Rotten enough for you not to speak to her now? You won't have another chance.'

Tess gnawed on her lip. 'I won't see her again?' she asked. 'Never?'

Lechasseur shook his head.

Again Tess shifted uncomfortably. 'Probably should then, shouldn't I?'

'That's up to you.'

'She probably won't want nothing to do with me,' Tess said sullenly. 'But I could say something to her.'

'Do you want to?'

Tess nodded.

Lechasseur put his hand in the small of Tess's back and gave her a slight push. 'Then you'd better go see her.'

The walk between Lechasseur and Joan should have taken just a few seconds, but Tess stopped after each step, uncomfortable and unsure of what she could say to this woman, the only real friend she had ever known. After an eternity, she found herself on the edge of Joan's group of women. She didn't recognise the faces of all the women, but she was certain she could name them.

'Sandi?' she asked a tall girl with straw-coloured hair, who was wearing a pair of flared jeans and a T-shirt that looked like a rainbow had been splashed across it.

'And I'd know you anywhere.' Sandi touched Tess' hair. 'I'd no idea you were so young.'

'We're all older than we look,' Joan Barton said. 'None of us is exactly who we seem to be,' she added, pointedly looking at Tess. Then she held up a hand to stop the girl speaking. 'Me included.' Her face softened. 'I shouldn't judge anyone. I don't have that right. No-one does.' There was still disapproval in the older woman's face, but now Tess couldn't tell if Joan's disappointment was in her or whether she felt a sense of failure in herself. Whatever the woman felt, it was clear that she was making an effort to reach out to Tess.

'I'm still pregnant,' Tess blurted. She had wondered what to say, and when the time came, that was all she had been able to manage, but it was enough. A look of relief cracked Joan's face, and she pulled the girl close into a great hug, exactly as she had done when they had first met in person. Tess felt that same feeling of security and warmth she'd felt before, but there was something else this time, too. A sadness in knowing that she would never again see this woman she loved more than she had ever loved her own mother. It was a loss she didn't want to think about.

Joan understood exactly the emotions that ran through Tess. Having lost her children, she was giving up the friends she had come to think of as a second family. 'It's all right,' she said, holding Tess at arms' length. 'You have that baby of yours to look after now, remember.'

Tess nodded. 'And he'll grow up to be a good boy, not spoiled like the way he is in here.' She hoped she sounded more confident than she felt.

Lechasseur tapped Emily on the arm. 'I must be going soft,' he grumbled. 'I kinda liked the girl.'

Emily wasn't paying attention. She was concentrating on the small boy, whose eyes were still glazed as he sought the paths to take the women back to their own times. 'Hurry up,' she whispered under her breath. 'Hurry up.'

Honoré sucked his teeth nervously. 'You wouldn't care to tell me exactly what's going on?'

Emily shook her head tightly.

'Didn't think so.'

'But if we don't get these women moved quickly, I don't think any of us will be getting home safely.'

'I really don't like the sound of that.'

Emily's face was taut with anxiety. 'Neither do I.'

Abruptly the boy's eyes snapped back into focus. For a moment,

Emily was sure her plan had been found out, but the boy still seemed in high spirits. 'They're going now,' he beamed. 'I'll miss them, but I can go and visit them all, can't I?' He watched as a matronly, ancient Roman woman began to fade from sight. 'I can go anywhere and see anyone. I'll be free again.'

Emily stuffed her hands into her coat pockets so that the boy couldn't see the way she had them clenched into nervous fists. She forced her voice to stay calm. 'That must be quite something. To have all of time and space waiting for you.'

'It is.' The girl in animal skins disappeared. 'Being trapped here has been a torture for me. It's like a human being told he can walk in only one direction for the rest of his life.' Another woman disappeared. 'That's not a life at all. Not a real one.'

'No,' Emily agreed. 'I don't imagine it is.'

'I could tell you who you really are,' the boy offered suddenly. 'I think I should give you something for helping me get free. All I'd have to do is reach out through time, and I could show you it all.'

The breath caught in Emily's throat. The offer had come from nowhere, and it had shaken her completely.

'What do you mean?' Lechasseur asked. 'You could let her see who she really is? Where she really comes from?'

'Oh, yes.' The boy bobbed his head cheerfully. 'I can show Emily her whole life.' He paused thoughtfully. 'Can I call you Emily? It isn't your real name, you know.'

'I – I know.' Emily stumbled over the words. 'At least, I guessed it wasn't. It would be a coincidence.'

The boy held out a hand. 'I can take you home, back to before … and you can find out your real name.'

'What are you waiting for?' Lechasseur blurted. 'Go. Find out who you are.' He swung Emily to face him. 'You'll never get another chance like this. Go and find out who you really are,' he urged.

The boy pushed his hand closer to Emily's. 'It won't hurt.'

Emily looked between Honoré and the boy, a terrible mask of anguish on her face. 'I can't,' she breathed.

'You have to,' Honoré urged. 'I'll deal with whatever's here. I …' He stopped as Emily shook her head, wretchedly.

'I can't,' she repeated in a hollow voice.

And Honoré understood. Whatever Emily's secret plan for getting the women home entailed, it meant that she couldn't take this chance to discover the truth about herself, to answer the questions that had eaten at her every day since she had first arrived in London. She was being offered her own life back, and she had to refuse. 'God, Emily. I'm so sorry.'

'What?' A suspicious frown had appeared on the boy's face. 'Why won't she accept?'

Honoré could see Emily floundering for an answer. 'She will,' he answered for her. 'Once the women are all safe.'

'If that's what she wants.' The boy was disappointed that he would be delayed in fully stretching out through time again, but returned himself to sending the women back to their rightful places. From the middle of the group, a small woman with a misshapen, crooked arm hanging limp by her side began to fade away.

Honoré squeezed Emily's arm, and they exchanged a brief but meaningful glance. Honoré's expression conveyed quiet sympathy and support, while in reply, Emily's face showed a grim acceptance that she wasn't going to find out the truth about herself – and a deep concern that her plan, whatever it was, would still be uncovered. Whatever happened to the women, Lechasseur was sure that Emily was convinced that the two of them would not survive this experience. The group of women in the room was thinning out as more disappeared, sent back to their own times, taking who knew what kind of mental scars with them from their time trapped in this hellish never-world. No matter how it affected them, Lechasseur reflected, they would be better able to deal with their troubles in their own times, surrounded by a familiar world. How he and Emily would deal with the troubles coming their way, he had no idea. He offered his friend a tight smile. She replied with the slightest shake of her head.

'This is boring.' The boy's petulant statement broke into their melancholy.

'What is?' Lechasseur asked, more harshly than he had intended.

'This.' The boy waved a hand at the room of women. 'It's taking ages for them all to go, and I want to be free now!'

'But you will keep to your end of the bargain,' Emily said firmly. 'You promised.' In taking the boy's appearance, the creature had adopted some of a child's mannerisms. With a little luck, Emily was sure she could continue to use that to keep it to its side of their agreement.

'All right,' the boy slouched. 'You don't have to go on about that. I'll do what I said. I'm just bored waiting, that's all.'

'Listen, kid,' Lechasseur offered. 'If you're as bored as that, why not save yourself some time by opening up a path back to the tower for Emily and me?'

The boy tutted. 'All right.'

It seemed a smart enough suggestion to Lechasseur. Keeping the kid – or whatever it really was – occupied for a few moments setting up a route back to 1995 might mean that he and Emily could escape after all. It was only when he saw the horrified expression on Emily's face that he realised that he had apparently made the worst mistake of his life.

A splinter of the creature's consciousness shot out towards the tower in 1995. This was the simplest of tasks, little more than the flexing of a muscle, but the tower was indistinct, drifting in and out of existence. Temporal energy pulsed and flowed around the tower, engulfing it in waves and then retreating and leaving the structure to ebb out of being. It took a dozen attempts to latch onto the tower and create the bridge for Emily and Lechasseur to use. For an instant, the creature wondered if the temporal energy was a by-product of the women returning home, as their time snakes and timelines settled back into place. But then the suspicion it had felt at Emily's refusal of its offer to discover the truth about herself returned. Having devoured John Raymond's time snake, the creature knew it should be able to break free at any time. The energy of a time snake was all it had needed to slip its bonds and set itself free. It began to slip through time. For a moment, it felt the familiar sensation of passing through the years, before a jolt hurled it back to 1995. It tried again, and was again repelled back to 1995. Over and over it tried to break through time, and on every occasion it was forced back.

The creature raged. It was still trapped – and it was certain that

Emily Blandish knew why.

Honoré looked through the door, which had swung open a few moments earlier. An inky void was all that he saw beyond it. 'Familiar?' he asked Emily.

She nodded. 'I had been hoping for something a little less …'

'Terrifying?' Honoré offered.

'Insubstantial,' Emily answered. 'But I'm not complaining. To be honest, I'm surprised we even have this.'

'What have you done?' The accusation was screeched in a child's high-pitched squeal. It echoed around the room, distorted by the last, fog-like remnants of the dissolving walls.

Emily kept her expression carefully neutral. 'What do you mean?' she asked.

The boy's face was almost scarlet with fury, and his hands were bunched into small fists. 'You've done something,' he squealed.

'Have I?' From the corner of her eye, Emily saw another woman disappear. If she could keep the boy occupied until they were all gone …

'What did you do?' the boy screamed. Hot, angry tears wet his cheeks.

Emily retained her calm façade. 'Exactly what we agreed,' she replied evenly. 'I offered you the time snake of a man who didn't want his life.' She paused. 'And you took it.'

'I know!' the boy howled.

Emily eyed the women. A dozen or more were still in the room. Unfortunately, Tess was one of them. She clung to Joan as they watched the confrontation between Emily and the little boy.

'You cheated,' the boy squeaked.

'No,' Emily said firmly. 'You got exactly what you asked for. It's your fault that you didn't think of the repercussions of your actions.'

'What do you mean?'

'Think about it,' Emily said, again glancing furtively at the rapidly-diminishing group of women. 'The man whose time snake you took leapt from the tower.'

One of the remaining women, dressed in a smart pinstripe business suit, pushed Patience aside. 'John?' she demanded. 'What about him?'

'Be quiet,' Emily snapped, then added, more gently: 'Please, Alice.'

Uncertainly, Alice consented. Emily saw the other remaining women close ranks around Alice, offering comfort. One by one, they were still continuing to disappear, returning to their own times and places. There were only half a dozen left now. She returned her gaze to the boy. 'When you took that man's time snake, it was as though he had never existed.'

The boy glared back defiantly. 'So?'

'You took the time snake from the end of his life, didn't you?'

'Yes.'

'When he leaped from the tower?' Emily pressed.

'Yes.' The boy sounded frustrated by the questioning.

'The tower he built,' Emily continued. 'But if he never existed, he could never have built the tower, so he couldn't have thrown himself off of it, and you couldn't have become trapped in it.'

'But he did jump,' he boy sniped. 'And I am trapped.'

'Yes,' Emily agreed. 'You are – but you can't be, because the place you're trapped in never existed.'

'That doesn't make sense,' the boy spat angrily. 'You're confusing me.'

'You've created a mistake in time,' Emily explained. 'A paradox. You're trapped in a place that can't exist because of what you did.'

The boy's voice rose in frustration. 'I don't understand.'

Lechasseur quietly sympathised.

Emily continued. 'If the place you were trapped in never existed, you can't be trapped. But you are trapped and it does exist – except you just made sure it never will exist. You've confused time, and time can't deal with that. It will snap back into place, with a single timeline.'

'What will happen to this place?' The boy looked close to tears. 'What will happen to me?'

Genuinely saddened, Emily hunkered down by the boy and grasped his arms. 'I don't know,' she answered. 'I really don't.'

A challenge came into the lad's faltering voice. 'If I'm trapped here, so are you.'

'I know,' Emily agreed steadily. It wasn't something she relished admitting, but there seemed little point in arguing about it. 'I hadn't thought much past getting you to send the women back to their own times.'

'You gave up your chance to get out so that they could go home?' The boy seemed genuinely surprised. 'Why did you do that?'

'Because someone had to help them?' Emily searched for a better answer but couldn't find one. 'They deserved better than to be trapped here.'

'They didn't all get away, though,' the boy sniffed. 'I didn't manage to send them all home.'

Emily swung round, to see that Tess and Joan were still left in the room, standing huddled together near the open door to the void, mixed expressions of confusion and fear on their faces. A terrible thought suddenly returned to Emily: if Tess was still there, so was her baby. Would or could this creature, knowing that it remained trapped, simply take the life of Tess's baby by force? Emily's mind raced. Giving up the baby wasn't an option, but there had to be an escape of some kind. There had to be.

The boy was looking at her, clearly puzzled by the worried expression on her face. 'What is it?'

Realising that she had to deflect the creature's thoughts away from Tess, she pulled the boy into a tight hug. 'The end will be quick, won't it?' she asked.

The boy's voice was muffled by her shoulder. 'I don't know.'

Emily was barely listening to the boy. Her eyes had latched onto the door beside Honoré and the inky void beyond it. If the creature had reached the tower, there was a chance for an escape that way. Behind the boy's back, she made a brisk circling gesture towards Tess and Joan with her hand, and then pointed to the door. She looked urgently towards Honoré, hoping that he had understood. The deeply uneasy expression that came over his face told Emily that he had. She silently mouthed the words, 'Go! Now!'

For a moment, Honoré looked set to argue, but then he reluctantly conceded. Holding a finger to his lips, he ushered the two women towards the door. They held back, unwilling to go back into the blackness they had inhabited for so long. 'It's okay,' Lechasseur said softly. 'It's not what it looks like. It's just a tunnel.' They weren't convinced. 'Okay,' he said ruefully. 'I guess I'm going first.'

'Not bloody likely.' Seeing that Lechasseur meant to do what he said, Tess grasped his arm, holding him back. 'If this really is a way out, we're having it.' Clasping Joan's hand, Tess hauled together her courage and plunged through the door into darkness, pulling Joan behind her.

'The baby!' The boy's head jerked up from Emily's shoulder. 'It's gone!'

Emily stiffened, desperately hoping that the boy wouldn't say that Tess had died in the abyss between this enclave and the tower.

The boy pulled away and stared at her accusingly. 'I could still have used it to get free.'

'I know,' Emily replied. 'Are they still alive?'

'Of course they're alive,' the boy grumbled. He sank to the floor and pulled his knees up tight under his chin. 'They made it across the bridge I created for you.' He glared at Emily. 'You tricked me.'

Emily had no answer. 'I didn't want to hurt you,' she said finally.

The boy choked out a humourless laugh. 'If you knew … I didn't want to hurt anybody, but I did.'

Lechasseur called from beside the door. 'Emily.' When she turned, he pointed meaningfully at the door.

'You can go,' the boy said bitterly. 'You don't have to make secret signals this time. I won't stop you.'

'Listen,' Emily said urgently. 'If there's a bridge, perhaps you can cross it and …'

'I have to stay here or it'll collapse,' the boy stated. 'Don't ask me to explain. You're not clever enough to understand it.'

'I don't want to leave you alone.'

'No doubt it won't be for long.'

'There must be another way,' Emily protested. 'There has to be.'

Lechasseur caught Emily's hand. 'There's no time,' he said, pulling her towards the door.

'We can't just leave him.'

'Look around, Emily,' Lechasseur demanded. 'This place won't be here much longer.'

He was right. Darkness was already breaking through one of the walls, and the contents of another room – Joan Barton's prized sitting room, Emily realised after a moment – were trying to pass through another.

'Emily.' Lechasseur yanked hard on her arm. 'We have to go – now!'

As she was pulled through the door, Emily turned and saw the small figure seated on the floor at the centre of a melting tumult. He shrugged at her, then looked away. Then Emily's view of the room blinked out, and she was in darkness.

CHAPTER TWELVE

Alice lurched forward and found herself in the familiar surroundings of the Dragon Industry Tower. She spun round, and looked at the sign on the door. *Giovanni Imports.* She was home. 'It worked,' she breathed. 'It sodding well worked. I'm home.' She slapped a wall hard, just to make sure. Her hand stung from the impact, and she relished the sharp pain that shot up her arm. It was real.

'I shouldn't do that if I was you.'

Alice spun round. Tess was standing behind her, arm-in-arm with Joan.

'What are you doing here?'

'Wondering where here is,' Tess snapped. 'An' you look like you know, so you can tell us.'

Alice eyed the familiar surroundings and wondered if Carol Fleming still worked in Giovanni Imports. How would her kids be doing now; especially Ellie, the eldest? People she had cut from her life and refused to talk to after John had died, she now wanted to see again. Maybe she could see Carol at the coffee shop for that espresso and the guilty pleasure of a blueberry muffin. She hoped it could happen. 'I'm home,' she said. 'My home.'

Tess was unimpressed. 'Weird looking home,' she said.

'No, it's not where I live, it's where I work.' Alice caught herself. 'Though there were times you could have thought I did live here.'

Two more figures stepped through the Giovanni Imports doors.

'It worked!' Lechasseur exclaimed.

'You sound as surprised as I feel,' Emily commented. She stopped in her tracks when she saw the small group of women standing there.

'I'd kind of hoped that those two would be back in their own times,' Lechasseur murmured, indicating Joan and Tess.

'No,' Emily shook her head. 'He – it – had stopped sending them back to their own times when you put them across that bridge.'

Suddenly, a bolt of blue lightning arced across the doorway and into the wall. Around them, the building pulsed slightly and slipped out of focus momentarily.

'Time's catching up with this place,' Emily said quickly. 'We don't have long before this building never existed.'

'In that case,' replied Lechasseur, 'I'd suggest we get out of here.'

Alice didn't argue, even though what they had said made no sense to her.

'This is your time?' Lechasseur asked briskly. Alice nodded. 'Good,' he continued. 'You can lead the way out.'

Reasoning that, as in a fire drill, it was safest not to use the lift, Alice hurriedly led the small party through a nearby swing door and into the stairwell. They then descended the stairs as fast as they could, while around them the building rumbled and lurched ominously.

After what seemed an age, they finally reached the ground floor, and emerged into the reception area. 'Probably best if we get outside,' Emily said. 'There's no way of knowing what's going to happen in here.' She looked around, wondering if there would be any sign of Dorkins, the security guard that she and Honoré had met earlier, but he was nowhere in sight. It was possible he wasn't in the building any more, his timeline already altered. She had no way of knowing. A crackle of energy arced across the reception area and shot through the wall right where Lechasseur had been standing. He managed to duck clear an instant before the energy hit.

'Time to leave.' Emily was already heading for the front door, pushing Joan, Tess and Alice ahead of her.

Emily had to jump to reach the top lock on the door, but on the second try, the door slid open automatically. Feeling Tess begin to take a step back, Emily planted a hand in the small of the girl's back and shoved hard. 'Outside,' she ordered firmly. She could see that the snow had continued falling all the time they had been inside the tower and was now several inches deep on the ground. That couldn't be helped. 'Stop over there under the light.' She pointed to one of the lights illuminating the car park. She gave Tess another push, and the girl tottered off in the direction she had indicated, Joan hanging onto her arm to stay upright on the slippery surface. Alice followed close behind, with Emily and Lechasseur bringing up the rear. Behind them, the crackles and sparks of energy had become bigger, and now arced their way around the building. By the time that Emily and Lechasseur reached the gathering point under the light, the entire tower was engulfed with sharp, blue lightning bolts shooting down, round and across the building, arcing from one side to another, imbuing the falling snow with an eerie blue colour. The blue electricity sparked faster and faster, and brighter and brighter.

'Close your eyes,' instructed Emily. The three women complied, Tess even covering her eyes with her hands and burying her head in Joan's shoulder.

The final flash was bright enough to be seen even through closed eyelids, and there was a soft sound and a rush of wind before they realised that they were standing in darkness.

Lechasseur was first to crack open his eyes. 'The light's gone,' he said.

Sure enough, the electric light under which they had been standing was gone. It wasn't just out – it simply wasn't there at all.

Emily peered into the snowy gloom. 'That's not all that's gone,' she said.

Behind them, where the tower had stood a few moments earlier, was a row of warehouses with the name BOLDMAN EXPORTS painted on their sides. The car park was also gone, and they were now standing in a large loading area surrounded by a chain-link fence.

'So the tower was never there?' Honoré asked Emily.

'No,' Emily replied. 'Then again, yes.' She grimaced. 'Oh, don't ask me. I'll only get a headache trying to work it out.

'Alice,' she called.

'Yes?'

'Were those warehouses there before the tower was built?'

'Yes, yes they were,' Alice answered. 'Boldman was an subsidiary of Dragon Industry. We kept smaller company names when we bought them over. Better PR with the local community.'

'So time has settled into place,' Emily said thoughtfully.

'Wait.' Alice sounded confused. 'If John Raymond never existed …' She waited to be corrected, but when neither Emily nor Lechasseur spoke, she continued: '… Why do I remember him?'

'We were outside of time when it set this new path,' Emily answered, 'so our memories weren't attuned to think of this path as being real and proper. We all keep our own memories.'

'Good,' Alice said firmly. 'I don't want to forget John. He deserved better than to be forgotten. And at least now perhaps his death served a purpose.'

Emily glanced across at Joan and Tess, huddled together nearby, shivering in the freezing weather. 'But they're trapped here,' she said. 'This isn't their home any more than that void was.'

Alice looked too, then moved over to join the stranded pair.

Emily turned to Honoré. 'What will they do, I wonder? We didn't do a very good job here, did we? We saved them from a safe prison and left them here.'

'We did our best,' Honoré said. 'We did the best we could, with the best of intentions.'

'That poor creature had the best of intentions, too,' Emily countered. 'And we know which road is littered with good intentions.'

Lechasseur felt his shoulders slump. Then he and Emily both swung round as they heard a high-pitched, electronic chiming noise. They saw Alice holding up to her ear a device that they recognised, from their recent adventure in Japan[3], as a mobile phone.

'Mum?' Alice was saying. 'Look, I know we haven't spoken in a while, but I was wondering if I could pop round to see you this evening. And, if you don't mind, I've got a couple of friends I'd like to bring with me …'

Lechasseur grinned. 'I don't know,' he reflected. 'Maybe things aren't going to turn out quite so bad after all.'

''Ere, what the hell are you lot doing there!'

3 See *Time Hunter: Kitsune.*

Lechasseur and Emily swung round again to see, striding toward them from the direction of the nearest Boldman Exports warehouse, the elderly, uniformed figure of Dorkins, the security guard.

'I guess some things haven't really changed all that much, either,' mused Lechasseur.

'We'll have time to think about that later,' replied Emily. 'Once we're back in 1950. Can you see Dorkins' time snake?'

'Sure can.'

'Okay then.'

Emily took Honoré's hand firmly in hers, and a moment later they were both gone, leaving only the faintest trace of blue lightning lingering momentarily in the air where they had stood.

After everything they'd experienced, Alice, Joan and Tess hardly blinked an eye at this. Dorkins, however, dropped to his knees in the snow, his jaw falling opening in astonishment. 'Bloody hell!' he breathed. 'They always said this place was haunted, but I never thought I'd see a pair of ghosts with my own two eyes!'

In the midst of the collapsing enclave it had built outside of time, the creature curled up and waited to die. It wanted to be angry with Emily; it wanted to hate her for tricking it and leaving it here, but it couldn't. It understood that she had done what she thought best for the women the creature had cared for. It didn't understand why she had refused to surrender the existence of a child, a being that wasn't alive yet. Among the creature's species, the unborn were an irrelevance. They became real only when they were born. But it didn't care now. It was tired and beaten and only wanted it all to end. Time snapped back and forth, establishing timelines, discarding false time tracks and erasing that which now had never happened. And all the time, the pocket the creature had built shrank under the onslaught from time, until it closed around the creature. The pain from the waves of time beating and tearing at it was almost unbearable, and the creature felt an enormous relief when a huge swell of temporal energy crashed into the battered remains of the enclave, wiping it away and erasing it from history. And then there was darkness.

And slowly, as the creature became aware again, amazed that it was still alive, small pin-pricks of light became clear in the darkness, and it felt a familiar sensation. It was free, floating in space between worlds. Those specks of light were far off stars it could visit. Tentatively, still afraid of being repelled again, the creature reached out through time and found no obstacles barring its path. Elation coursed through its being, and the creature began to slide exultantly through time. It was free.

ABOUT THE AUTHOR

Claire Bartlett does not exist. She was created by Iain McLaughlin to take the flack if people hated his work. So, to be clear, she did not graduate with a teaching degree; she is not the assistant editor of *Animals And You* magazine and she has not co-written *Doctor Who* short stories and two scripts for a *Doctor Who* audio spin off range. So, if you meet someone claiming to be Claire Bartlett, see a doctor, you're imagining things.

Iain McLaughlin does not exist. He is a figment of Claire Bartlett's imagination, created on one of her less happy days, and he is, in fact, a pseudonym. So, should you see him in the bar at a convention, ignore him. He's not really there. He has not written plays and short stories and did not write *Blood And Hope*, a *Doctor Who* novella for Telos.

Claire Bartlett would like you to know that she did breed penguins in Alaska for a year before moving on to koala-farming, while Iain McLaughlin's claim to fame is that he cut the toenails of the Tibetan monks in Nepal.

Neither Claire Bartlett nor Iain McLaughlin actually exists. Probably. And they certainly shouldn't be allowed to write their biographies in the pub.

* Some of the above might not be 100% accurate.

ACKNOWLEDGEMENTS

Thanks to George Mann and David Howe for making it work.

And special thanks to our families and friends. The best.

TIME HUNTER

A range of high-quality, original paperback and limited edition hardback novellas featuring the adventures in time of Honoré Lechasseur. Part mystery, part detective story, part dark fantasy, part science fiction ... these books are guaranteed to enthral fans of good fiction everywhere, and are in the spirit of our acclaimed range of *Doctor Who* Novellas.

ALREADY AVAILABLE

THE WINNING SIDE by LANCE PARKIN

Emily is dead! Killed by an unknown assailant. Honoré and Emily find themselves caught up in a plot reaching from the future to their past, and with their very existence, not to mention the future of the entire world, at stake, can they unravel the mystery before it is too late?
An adventure in time and space.
£7.99 (+ £1.50 UK p&p) Standard p/b ISBN 1-903889-35-9 (pb)
£25.00 (+ £1.50 UK p&p) Deluxe h/b ISBN 1-903889-36-7 (hb)

THE TUNNEL AT THE END OF THE LIGHT by STEFAN PETRUCHA

In the heart of post-war London, a bomb is discovered lodged at a disused station between Green Park and Hyde Park Corner. The bomb detonates, and as the dust clears, it becomes apparent that *something* has been awakened. Strange half-human creatures attack the workers at the site, hungrily searching for anything containing sugar ...

Meanwhile, Honoré and Emily are contacted by eccentric poet Randolph Crest, who believes himself to be the target of these subterranean creatures. The ensuing investigation brings Honoré and Emily up against a terrifying force from deep beneath the earth, and one which even with their combined powers, they may have trouble stopping.
An adventure in time and space.
£7.99 (+ £1.50 UK p&p) Standard p/b ISBN 1-903889-37-5 (pb)
£25.00 (+ £1.50 UK p&p) Deluxe h/b ISBN 1-903889-38-3 (hb)

THE CLOCKWORK WOMAN by CLAIRE BOTT

Honoré and Emily find themselves imprisoned in the 19th Century by a celebrated inventor … but help comes from an unexpected source – a humanoid automaton created by and to give pleasure to its owner. As the trio escape to London, they are unprepared for what awaits them, and at every turn it seems impossible to avert what fate may have in store for the Clockwork Woman.

An adventure in time and space.

£7.99 (+ £1.50 UK p&p) Standard p/b ISBN 1-903889-39-1 (pb)
£25.00 (+ £1.50 UK p&p) Deluxe h/b ISBN 1-903889-40-5 (hb)

KITSUNE by JOHN PAUL CATTON

In the year 2020, Honoré and Emily find themselves thrown into a mystery, as an ice spirit – *Yuki-Onna* – wreaks havoc during the Kyoto Festival, and a haunted funhouse proves to contain more than just paper lanterns and wax dummies. But what does all this have to do with the elegant owner of the Hide and Chic fashion chain … and to the legendary Chinese fox-spirits, the Kitsune?

An adventure in time and space.

£7.99 (+ £1.50 UK p&p) Standard p/b ISBN 1-903889-41-3 (pb)
£25.00 (+ £1.50 UK p&p) Deluxe h/b ISBN 1-903889-42-1 (hb)

THE SEVERED MAN by GEORGE MANN

What links a clutch of sinister murders in Victorian London, an angel appearing in a Staffordshire village in the 1920s and a small boy running loose around the capital in 1950? When Honoré and Emily encounter a man who appears to have been cut out of time, they think they have the answer. But soon enough they discover that the mystery is only just beginning and that nightmares can turn into reality.

An adventure in time and space.

£7.99 (+ £1.50 UK p&p) Standard p/b ISBN 1-903889-43-X (pb)
£25.00 (+ £1.50 UK p&p) Deluxe h/b ISBN 1-903889-44-8 (hb)

COMING SOON

PECULIAR LIVES by PHILIP PURSER HALLARD

An adventure in time and space.

£7.99 (+ £1.50 UK p&p) Standard p/b ISBN 1-903889-47-2 (pb)
£25.00 (+ £1.50 UK p&p) Deluxe h/b ISBN 1-903889-48-0 (hb)
PUB: JULY 2005 (UK)

TIME HUNTER FILM

DAEMOS RISING by DAVID J HOWE, DIRECTED BY KEITH BARNFATHER

Daemos Rising is a sequel to both the *Doctor Who* adventure *The Daemons* and to *Downtime*, an earlier drama featuring the Yeti. It is also a prequel of sorts to Telos Publishing's *Time Hunter* series. It stars Miles Richardson as ex-UNIT operative Douglas Cavendish, and Beverley Cressman as Brigadier Lethbridge-Stewart's daughter Kate. Trapped in an isolated cottage, Cavendish thinks he is seeing ghosts. The only person who might understand and help is Kate Lethbridge-Stewart … but when she arrives, she realises that Cavendish is key in a plot to summon the Daemons back to the Earth. With time running out, Kate discovers that sometimes even the familiar can turn out to be your worst nightmare. Also starring Andrew Wisher, and featuring Ian Richardson as the Narrator.
An adventure in time and space.
£14.00 (+ £2.50 UK p&p) PAL format R4 DVD
Order direct from Reeltime Pictures, PO Box 23435, London SE26 5WU

HORROR/FANTASY

CAPE WRATH by PAUL FINCH

Death and horror on a deserted Scottish island as an ancient Viking warrior chief returns to life.
£8.00 (+ £1.50 UK p&p) Standard p/b ISBN: 1-903889-60-X

KING OF ALL THE DEAD by STEVE LOCKLEY & PAUL LEWIS

The king of all the dead will have what is his.
£8.00 (+ £1.50 UK p&p) Standard p/b ISBN: 1-903889-61-8

GUARDIAN ANGEL by STEPHANIE BEDWELL-GRIME

Devilish fun as Guardian Angel Porsche Winter loses a soul to the devil …
£9.99 (+ £2.50 UK p&p) Standard p/b ISBN: 1-903889-62-6

FALLEN ANGEL by STEPHANIE BEDWELL-GRIME

Porsche Winter battles she devils on Earth …
£9.99 (+ £2.50 UK p&p) Standard p/b ISBN: 1-903889-69-3

ASPECTS OF A PSYCHOPATH by ALISTAIR LANGSTON

Goes deeper than ever before into the twisted psyche of a serial killer.
Horrific, graphic and gripping, this book is not for the squeamish.
£8.00 (+ £1.50 UK p&p) Standard p/b ISBN: 1-903889-63-4

SPECTRE by STEPHEN LAWS

The inseparable Byker Chapter: six boys, one girl, growing up
together in the back streets of Newcastle. Now memories are all that
Richard Eden has left, and one treasured photograph. But suddenly,
inexplicably, the images of his companions start to fade, and as they
vanish, so his friends are found dead and mutilated. Something is
stalking the Chapter, picking them off one by one, something
connected with their past, and with the girl they used to know.
£9.99 (+ £2.50 UK p&p) Standard p/b ISBN: 1-903889-72-3

THE HUMAN ABSTRACT by GEORGE MANN

A future tale of private detectives, AIs, Nanobots, love and death.
£7.99 (+ £1.50 UK p&p) Standard p/b ISBN: 1-903889-65-0

BREATHE by CHRISTOPHER FOWLER

The Office meets *Night of the Living Dead.*
£7.99 (+ £1.50 UK p&p) Standard p/b ISBN: 1-903889-67-7
£25.00 (+ £1.50 UK p&p) Deluxe h/b ISBN: 1-903889-68-5

HOUDINI'S LAST ILLUSION by STEVE SAVILE

Can master illusionist Harry Houdini outwit the dead shades of his past?
£7.99 (+ £1.50 UK p&p) Standard p/b ISBN: 1-903889-66-9

ALICE'S JOURNEY BEYOND THE MOON by R J CARTER

A sequel to the classic Lewis Carroll tales.
£6.99 (+ £1.50 UK p&p) Standard p/b ISBN: 1-903889-76-6
£30.00 (+ £1.50 UK p&p) Deluxe h/b ISBN: 1-903889-77-4

APPROACHING OMEGA by ERIC BROWN

A colonisation mission to Earth runs into problems.
£7.99 (+ £1.50 UK p&p) Standard p/b ISBN: 1-903889-98-7
£30.00 (+ £1.50 UK p&p) Deluxe h/b ISBN: 1-903889-99-5

TV/FILM GUIDES

A DAY IN THE LIFE: THE UNOFFICIAL AND UNAUTHORISED GUIDE TO 24 by KEITH TOPPING

Complete episode guide to the first season of the popular TV show.
£9.99 (+ £2.50 p&p) Standard p/b ISBN: 1-903889-53-7

THE TELEVISION COMPANION: THE UNOFFICIAL AND UNAUTHORISED GUIDE TO DOCTOR WHO by DAVID J HOWE & STEPHEN JAMES WALKER

Complete episode guide to the popular TV show.
£14.99 (+ £4.75 UK p&p) Standard p/b ISBN: 1-903889-51-0

LIBERATION: THE UNOFFICIAL AND UNAUTHORISED GUIDE TO BLAKE'S 7 by ALAN STEVENS & FIONA MOORE

Complete episode guide to the popular TV show.
Featuring a foreword by David Maloney
£9.99 (+ £2.50 UK p&p) Standard p/b ISBN: 1-903889-54-5

HOWE'S TRANSCENDENTAL TOYBOX: SECOND EDITION by DAVID J HOWE & ARNOLD T BLUMBERG

Complete guide to *Doctor Who* Merchandise.
£25.00 (+ £4.75 UK p&p) Standard p/b ISBN: 1-903889-56-1

HOWE'S TRANSCENDENTAL TOYBOX: 2003 EDITION by DAVID J HOWE & ARNOLD T BLUMBERG

Complete guide to *Doctor Who* Merchandise released in 2003.
£7.99 (+ £1.50 UK p&p) Standard p/b ISBN: 1-903889-57-X

A VAULT OF HORROR by KEITH TOPPING

A Guide to 80 Classic (and not so classic) British Horror Films

£12.99 (+ £4.75 UK p&p) Standard p/b ISBN: 1-903889-58-8

BEAUTIFUL MONSTERS: THE UNOFFICIAL AND UNAUTHORISED GUIDE TO THE ALIEN AND PREDATOR FILMS by DAVID McINTEE

A Guide to the *Alien* and *Predator* Films

£9.99 (+ £2.50 UK p&p) Standard p/b ISBN: 1-903889-94-4

THE HANDBOOK: THE UNOFFICIAL AND UNAUTHORISED GUIDE TO THE PRODUCTION OF DOCTOR WHO by DAVID J HOWE, STEPHEN JAMES WALKER and MARK STAMMERS

Complete guide to the making of *Doctor Who*.

£14.99 (+ £4.75 UK p&p) Standard p/b ISBN: 1-903889-59-6

£30.00 (+ £4.75 UK p&p) Deluxe h/b ISBN: 1-903889-96-0

HANK JANSON

Classic pulp crime thrillers from the 1940s and 1950s.

TORMENT by HANK JANSON

£9.99 (+ £1.50 UK p&p) Standard p/b ISBN: 1-903889-80-4

WOMEN HATE TILL DEATH by HANK JANSON

£9.99 (+ £1.50 UK p&p) Standard p/b ISBN: 1-903889-81-2

SOME LOOK BETTER DEAD by HANK JANSON

£9.99 (+ £1.50 UK p&p) Standard p/b ISBN: 1-903889-82-0

SKIRTS BRING ME SORROW by HANK JANSON

£9.99 (+ £1.50 UK p&p) Standard p/b ISBN: 1-903889-83-9

WHEN DAMES GET TOUGH by HANK JANSON

£9.99 (+ £1.50 UK p&p) Standard p/b ISBN: 1-903889-85-5

ACCUSED by HANK JANSON

£9.99 (+ £1.50 UK p&p) Standard p/b ISBN: 1-903889-86-3

KILLER by HANK JANSON

£9.99 (+ £1.50 UK p&p) Standard p/b ISBN: 1-903889-87-1

FRAILS CAN BE SO TOUGH by HANK JANSON

£9.99 (+ £1.50 UK p&p) Standard p/b ISBN: 1-903889-88-X

THE TRIALS OF HANK JANSON by STEVE HOLLAND

£12.99 (+ £2.50 UK p&p) Standard p/b ISBN: 1-903889-84-7

The prices shown are correct at time of going to press. However, the publishers reserve the right to increase prices from those previously advertised without prior notice.

TELOS PUBLISHING
c/o Beech House, Chapel Lane, Moulton, Cheshire, CW9 8PQ, England
Email: orders@telos.co.uk
Web: www.telos.co.uk

To order copies of any Telos books, please visit our website where there are full details of all titles and facilities for worldwide credit card online ordering, or send a cheque or postal order (UK only) for the appropriate amount (including postage and packing), together with details of the book(s) you require, plus your name and address to the above address. Overseas readers please send two international reply coupons for details of prices and postage rates.